JINGLE ME BALLS

SEA SHENANIGANS, BOOK 6

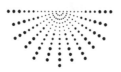

ROBYN PETERMAN

ACKNOWLEDGMENTS

The Sea Shenanigans Series has been an absolute joy to write. I've laughed like a loon while writing this particular series. Since I was little I'd always wanted to be a Mermaid. Of course, that is impossible so I did the next best thing. I wrote about them. LOL
Jingle Me Balls is the hilarious conclusion to the six book series and it's a doozy. Poseidon is one of my favorite characters and it was time for his story. I hope you enjoy reading it as much as I enjoyed writing it.

As always, there are many people who help me out along the way. While writing is a solitary job, it takes many wonderful people to get the book into the readers hands. I am a very lucky gal to have such amazing people in my corner.

Wanda, you rock hard. Thank you.

Sara Lunsford. thank you. Your editing saved me from hilariously embarrassing mistakes.

Renee George, thank you. You are my Best Cookie forever.

My readers, thank you. I write because I have to or I'd go nuts. LOL However, the fact that my books are loved by you makes it all worth it.

My family, thank you. None of this would be any fun without you. I love you.

DEDICATION

For Wanda. This one is for you.

BOOK DESCRIPTION

What in the salty seas could be more important than *presents* at Christmas time?
Nothing. Absolutely nothing.

Tis' Christmas time on Mystical Isle and just like the fat bastard in red, I've made a list and now I shall check it...*twice*. Yeah, twice. I might wear a diaper, but I'm not an arse.

Battle the human women in sweatpants and snow boots for electronics on Black Friday. Check.

Cover each palm tree in lights even though the Mermaids insist they look phallic. Check. By the way, what does phallic mean? Never mind. Check.

Moving on.

Weave a Christmas tale during family story time on the beach, have a family portrait made in the special sweaters I pilfered, and write a letter to Santa. I mean, fat bastard… Check.

Planning activities that may end in bloodshed. Check. That's what I call a yuletide win, so check-check.

The Mermaids have baked lovely Christmas cookies that will go wonderfully with the rum in my diaper. And everyone has voted to veto caroling since Pirate Doug has a singing voice that can kill… literally. The present exchange would be ruined if everyone was dead. Could my days be merrier or brighter? Uh, no. Check.

It seems I have *everything* under control and Christmas on Mystical Isle will be unforgettable, or I'm not the Well-Hung God of the Sea, Poseidon.
 And I am. Check.

THE THRONE ROOM... MINE'S BIGGER

"THAT WAS CERTAINLY A SHITESHOW AND A HALF," I SAID, pulling a bottle of rum from my diaper and taking a healthy swig.

"Yes, Poseidon it was," Wally said, looking down at me from her enormous jewel- encrusted throne. "We are *never* inviting all of your children to Thanksgiving again. At least five hundred of the nine hundred and whatever showed up. The palace is a disaster."

My mate was correct. All three hundred and thirteen rooms in our palace had been ransacked by my inebriated offspring. While it was heartwarming to see them all so soused while violently wrestling each other, they were somewhat out of control—especially the girls.

"Thank the Seven Seas not everyone came," I said, trying to figure out what was bothering me right now. I had a strange feeling that something wasn't quite right. "However, my favorite part of the evening was when Zeus popped his head in to say hello, and someone yelled *food fight*. Did my heart good to see the arsehole get beaned with hundreds of pumpkin pies."

"That was you, darling," Wally said, trying to bite back a grin. *"You* yelled *food fight."*

My dark-haired beauty with the outstanding left hook and tremendous knockers was my reason for living. My alarmingly large army of children came next with rum coming in at a solid third. Of course, my job was a joy. Being the well-hung God of the Sea came with great pay and even greater perks. The Royal Palace on Mt. Olympus was just one such perk. However, there was definitely something odd going on in the throne room at the moment.

"Do you think Zeus could tell it was me?" I asked with a chuckle, glancing around the opulent room to spy if any of my offspring might have passed out and were still here.

Nope. All clear.

"Definitely," Wally said with an eye roll. "I'm quite sure when you shouted *'My spawn, as your father, Poseidon, I command you to throw pie at the pecker standing in the doorway'* was a dead giveaway."

"Shite," I muttered, taking another swig. "The sneaky bastard will try to get me back."

"Not to worry," Wally said with a naughty little smile. "I have his throne. If he messes with you, I'll paint it hot pink."

"That's what's wrong," I said, glancing up in shock at my violent gal. "You're seated at least three feet higher than I am."

"That I am," Wally said with a wink that made my roger jolly.

"As much as I enjoy looking up your dress—and I defi-nitely do," I said with a grin, getting ready to duck just in case I put my foot into my mouth and pulled it out of my arse, as my mate liked to say. "Makes my Johnson feel a bit deflated when your throne is bigger than mine."

"I won it in the poker game the other night," Wally said.

"Strip poker?" I bellowed. If the other gods had seen Wally's melons, I'd have to kill them. That could get a bit dicey since we were all extremely hard to kill.

"Of course not," she said with a laugh. "I'd have to bleach my eyes if I ever saw Hades' privates. Regular poker. I won fair and square."

"You didn't threaten them?" I asked, impressed that my gal had beat the old codgers.

"Maybe a bit," Wally said with a delighted laugh.

Gods, I adored my woman. "What would it take to trade thrones?"

"Not much," she said with a grin that looked so innocent it terrified me.

"Mmmkay," I said, downing the rest of the bottle. "Define *not much*."

Wally stepped off the throne, moved to where I sat, and straddled me. It was pretty much a done deal that my nutty gal was going to get whatever she wanted.

"I want to spend Christmas on Mystical Isle with our idiot son, Pirate Doug, and his lovely mate, Tallulah. I adore all the Mermaids there and Mt. Olympus is so stuffy and boring," she said. "Plus, the resort the girls run is absolutely divine."

3

I didn't even have to think about it. The plan was brilliant.

"Love it," I bellowed. "Besides, DIC is killing me. I'd like to just quit DIC—eliminate DIC altogether."

Wally closed her eyes and pressed her temples. "If you remove your Johnson, I'm out of here."

"Not my dick," I said with a laugh. "DIC."

"Clear as mud," she muttered.

"Divine Immortal Circuit. You know that all the gods have to take a turn governing the other idiots. If I hadn't lost at strip poker a few months back, I wouldn't have to run the damn thing for the next century. They are a bunch of whiney little shites."

"Right," she said, heaving a sigh of relief. "Well, in that case, I say we leave tonight. We can stay on Mystical Isle for the month. It will be a vacation!"

"Outstanding," I shouted as I scooped my she-devil into my arms and prepared to transport us to Mystical Isle. "And tomorrow is Black Friday."

"What in the world is Black Friday?" Wally asked.

"A day for a deal, my love. And I plan to deal."

2

BLACK FRIDAY... JUST SAY NO

"So that's the plan, boys," I bellowed, staring at the blank and confused faces of my men.

"You can't be serious," Cupid said with an eye roll. "We'll all die."

As we stood on the sandy beach of the Mystical Isle at 4 a.m., I doubted myself for only three-fourths of a second. Cupid—while he may be a demigod—was a pain in my arse and wouldn't know an excellent idea if it punched him in the head... which I was tempted to do. However, starting the day with bloodshed probably wasn't prudent. I needed every man on deck if my plan to come back with twenty blenders and vacuum cleaners was to come to fruition. Plus, I was still a bit bruised from the Thanksgiving wrestling match. My daughters had kicked my arse.

"You're immortal, and unless we run into middle-aged human women who are keen on decapitation, we'll be fine," I pointed out. "Don't be a squinch."

"A what?" Cupid asked, eyeing me in confusion.

"A squinch, ye cod-faced tar stain," Upton, the scrawny Pirate, explained to Cupid in my defense. "It's a wee arch built across the interior angle of two scurvy walls—usually to support a poop deck."

"Wait," I said perplexed. "Are you sure?"

"Nay," the little Pirate replied with a yawn. "I'm Upton."

"Okay, that's not what I meant then," I said. "What I *meant* to say was don't be such a winch."

"Have you been drinking?" Del inquired with a raised brow.

My Genie son was usually on my side, but I was feeling slightly ganged up on at the moment.

"Of course, I've been drinking," I huffed. "Need to get the blood moving. And yes, I meant a winch... I think. Upton, would you be so kind as to interpret for me so I can determine if that is indeed what I meant?"

"T'would be me pleasure, yar Majesty," Upton said, bowing low. It looked like the Pirate was going to take a dump, but it was the respect that mattered, not the visual. "Avast ye! The greatest and only God of the Sea—Poseidon, has spoken. A winch be the liftin' device consistin' of a horizontal cylinder turned by a galley hoppin' crank on which a cable of hempin' halter winds—usually kept in the dungbie."

"In your arse?" Pirate Doug asked with a horrified expression. "You keep that in your arse?"

"Nay," Upton said with a chuckle. "The dungbie of the ship—not in yar arse."

"Well, shite," I muttered. "That's not right, either. What I'm trying to say has nothing to do with putting any kind of object in your arse. Help a god out here... I'm talking about the hairy green guy with the dog who steals the ham."

"What the fuck?" Rick the Werewolf said, shaking his head. "Are you wasted?"

"Not until 10 a.m.," I told him. Normally, I liked Rick. He was insane and addicted to death-defying hobbies. Right now? Not so much. "That's hours away. You idiots must know who I'm talking about. He bursts out of his clothes when his internal organ grows."

"The Hulk?" Pirate Doug volunteered.

I could always count on my imbecile son's support. Most of the time, his support was embarrassing and profane. However, the effort was appreciated.

"No," I replied. "Not the Hulk."

"Any more obscure hints?" Cupid inquired.

"Hang on," I muttered as I paced the beach and tried to remember the damned name. "Lives in a cave. Likes to sew puffy white globules onto red jackets that support his beer gut. You must know who I'm talking about. He's famous."

"I am so confused," Keith the Selkie said, scratching his head. "I still don't understand why I got yanked out of bed to talk about globules and arses."

"That's not why I roused your sorry arses from your slumber," I shouted. "We're going Black Friday shopping for our women. We will get excellent deals on electrical merchandise and we will spend quality time together as a family. Nothing says I want to get into your pants like a self-cleaning crockpot."

"You've lost your damn mind," Del said with a laugh.

"Your point?" I demanded. My sanity had been in question for centuries. If my boy wanted to insult me, he was going to have to do better than that.

"No point. Just an observation, Pappy," Del replied.

Glancing at the motley crew, I sighed. Where was their holiday spirit? The only one who had been silent thus far was Bonar the Pirate. I was fairly sure he was asleep standing up. I'd chosen my shopping posse with care. My two sons, Pirate Doug and Del, had no choice. I was their father and would make their lives more of a living hell than usual if they refused me.

And the rest—Keith the Selkie with the maturity level of a fourth-grade boy, Rick the Werewolf with a death wish, and Cupid the pompous arse—were mated to the Mermaids I considered daughters. Well, not Bonar or Upton. The two Pirates were loyal and small. I figured they could pilfer items from carts of unsuspecting shoppers if the need arose. From all I'd read, the self-cleaning crockpots were a very hot ticket this year.

"We'll leave as soon as we discover what I'm talking about," I announced to a round of groans. "The hairy green son-of-a-bitch put horns on the head of his small beast."

"He put trumpets on his man tool?" Pirate Doug asked, perking up. "Tis a fine idea. I might do that myself."

I couldn't help myself. Punching Doug in the head was necessary. My boy had a hard head and was back on his feet almost immediately.

"They were no musical instruments on his Johnson. That's ridiculous," I bellowed, wondering if the idea was truly that bad. Wally might be impressed... although I'd need a tuba to compete with my salami. "He put antlers on his dog."

"That sounds kind of mean," Rick commented. Rick was a vegan Werewolf and had amassed quite the zoo of stray animals on the island.

"Well, the hairy green bastard is mean until the end of the cartoon," I explained, not wanting Rick to get his panties in a wad. I needed him. I had a sneaking suspicion that procuring the crockpots might be tricky. I needed someone willing to light themselves on fire as a distraction if necessary.

"Wait," Cupid said, shaking his head. "The hairy green bastard isn't a real person?"

"How should I know?" I said, throwing my hands in the air. "I'm sure he's based on a real person. I mean, he sounded like a real person on TV."

"This could take a month," Del said, sitting down in the sand and getting comfortable.

"Holy hell and seashells," Tallulah hissed as she marched out of the resort and stomped across the sand. "Why are you people awake, and what's going on here?"

"Tallulah, my purple hooker of love," Pirate Doug said, running to his mate's side. "We're playing a game with Pappy."

"Did you just call me a hooker?" she demanded, slapping her hands on her hips as everyone ran for cover.

"Umm... yes?" Pirate Doug whispered terrified.

"What have we discussed about calling Mermaids hookers?" she questioned her idiot.

"That we can?" Pirate Doug answered, still whispering.

"Nope," she said, decking the love of her immortal life. "We said no calling Mermaids hookers. Am I clear?"

"You are, my sexy hellcat," Pirate Doug said, hopping back to his feet and pumping his fists in the air. "My gal can punch like a freight train."

His pride in his mate's right hook warmed my heart. My Wally was a violent she-devil as well. The men in my line liked their women wild.

"Okay, everyone can come out of hiding," Tallulah called out and turned her attention to me. "What is going on, Poseidon?"

"It's a surprise," I told one of my favorite little Mermaids. "You will be quite thrilled. However, if you happen to know the name of the hairy green fucker who has a dog and steals hams, you could save me a tremendous amount of time."

"The Grinch," she said as she gave Pirate Doug a kiss and walked sleepily back to the resort.

"That's it," I shouted, dancing a little jig on the beach. I had no clue why I'd needed the damn name in the first place, but now that I had it the boys and I could go on our adventure.

"Where are we going to do this Black Friday?" Keith asked, still looking confused.

"Excellent question, Keith. As we're smack in the middle of the Bermuda Triangle right now, I figured Florida would be the closest place to shop," I announced.

"Umm... no can do," Pirate Doug said. "I have several warrants out for my arrest in that fair state."

"Twenty-nine," Upton volunteered, only to be sucker-punched by Pirate Doug.

Bonar was still sleeping standing up.

"Georgia?" I suggested.

"Nope," Pirate Doug replied sheepishly.

"Texas?" I tried again.

Keith raised his hand.

"Yes, Keith?" I asked.

"I might or might not have paid my excessive amount of parking tickets there. Since I'm not sure, I'd rather stay out of Texas."

"Fair enough," I said with an eye roll.

"Tennessee?" I asked.

"Nope," Pirate Doug said.

"Forty-nine warrants," Upton said with a grin as he ducked a right hook from Pirate Doug.

Blowing out a long and put-upon breath, I shook my head. This was getting complicated.

"Where *can* you shop?" I asked my idiot son.

"I know just the spot," Pirate Doug said as everyone looked on in what I perceived as fear.

Rolling my eyes, I gathered the group into a circle. I could transport all of us as long as I knew where we were going.

"Could you be a bit more specific?" I inquired as I raised my scepter high in the air in preparation for the trip.

"North Dakota," Pirate Doug announced. "Not a single warrant out in that state for my arrest."

"Where exactly is North Dakota?" I asked. My geography wasn't the best when it came to the human world. I spent most of my time boinking Wally and making the other god's lives hell on Mt. Olympus.

"North," Cupid said with a shudder. "Very north."

"To North Dakota we go!" I shouted as I waved my scepter in a circular motion and we were whipped into a magical windstorm.

I mean, how bad could North Dakota be?

"WHAT THE FUCK?" I SHOUTED AS I STOOD IN A FOOT OF snow outside of a department store known for carrying appliances. "I'm not dressed for this weather."

"Dude," Cupid said with a laugh. "You're wearing a diaper. You're not dressed at all."

"Your point?" I demanded. The lack of respect from these dumbarses was beginning to wear thin. "I look fabulous."

"Whatever you say," Cupid replied with a shrug.

Bonar woke up with a start and a loud scream of terror when we all landed in a snowbank. Taking a peek around, he began to mutter some kind of nonsense I decided to ignore.

"No shirt. No Shoes. No service," Bonar said.

"What?" I finally asked since he'd mumbled it eight times in a row.

"No shirt. No shoes. No service," he repeated once again.

"That's nice," I said, patting him on the head. The poor man had clearly been having a nightmare. "Alright, gentlemen and Pirate Doug, I have one hundred gold coins for each of you to spend today."

"I don't need gold coins," Pirate Doug announced with

pride. "I plan to pilfer the self-cleaning crockpot for Tallulah. It will mean more to her if it's stolen."

"Idiot," I yelled, backhanding him in the head and sending him flying. "We will not be banned from North Dakota by your unlawful deeds. That being said, I never want to come here again. So, if the gold coins don't cover the cost, I'm good with sticky fingers."

"The gold coins aren't worth shite," Rick said with a grin. "Not legal tender in North Dakota."

Del laughed and let his chin fall to his chest. "Pappy, gold coins don't work as money in human stores. Did you bring a credit card?

"What in the salty sea is a *credit card*, and what kind of *heathens* are these humans?" I shouted, causing a small avalanche of snow to land on all of us.

Keith politely raised his hand. I was impressed with his manners. However, I was a wee bit concerned he was about to announce that he remembered he had outstanding parking tickets in North Dakota. The clock was ticking. I'd read if you didn't get in early, you didn't get shite.

"Yes, Keith?"

"I have an idea," he said.

"Does it have anything to do with traffic violations?" I inquired.

"Umm… no," he replied.

"Fine," I huffed. "Spit it out. We need to get moving. There are only a limited amount of fucking self-cleaning crockpots to be had."

"We could put stuff on layaway and come back every

week with some of the money until it's paid off," Keith volunteered.

"How do you know of this bizarre method?" I demanded. I really didn't ever want to set foot in North Dakota again. My nuts were frozen. However, if the layaway business would keep us from being incarcerated in a human pokey, it might have merit.

"I saw it on the Brady Bunch," Keith explained.

"And this bunch of Brady people… did they not possess the mystical credit card either?" I asked.

"Umm… no. Not as far as I know," Keith confirmed.

"Fine," I said. "We will use the bunch of Brady layaway method. Gentlemen, this could be a dangerous mission. If anyone would like a swig of rum before we go in, I've got three bottles stored next to my impressive junk."

Surprisingly no one took me up on my offer.

Pointing to the buildings in front of us, I devised the strategy. "There have to be a least twenty emporiums to procure electronics, men. We will spread out and work quickly. I'd suggest that no man go alone. Human women are known to be grabby and vicious on the holiday of Black Friday."

"Black Friday is a holiday?" Rick asked.

"Shut up," I snapped. This was not a good time to blast Rick with a bolt of lightning. He was my main soldier of distraction. "Cupid, be prepared to shoot your arrows at people who are too close to the self-cleaning crockpots. If they're busy falling in love, they'll forget about the precious booty we're after. Keith, you can communicate with Krakens and other violent sea creatures… this may come in handy with savage human women. Be prepared to use your skills."

Everyone looked confused. No matter. It was still quite early in the morning. They would get the hang of it once we were in the middle of battle.

"Rick, be ready to set yourself ablaze. I think a smallish inferno would clear a boutique quite nicely," I said. I was sure I heard snickers, but they wouldn't be laughing if we were attacked by ferocious, blood-thirsty shoppers. They would thank me for my outstanding game plan. "Del, use your magic carpet if need be. You can swipe items from carts and fly away. It's genius. Bonar and Upton, be prepared to lift electronics from shopping carts of crazed women who have what we want. You're small, and I'd suggest that you belly crawl through the establishments. Keep a watchful eye out so you're not run over by the wheeled metal contraptions that the ruthless human females will be wielding. Pirate Doug?"

"Yes, Pappy?" he asked.

"Umm… try to stay out of trouble," I told him.

"We're all going to die," Cupid muttered with an eye roll.

"Bad attitude," I bellowed. "If you want a self-cleaning crockpot, you will have to fight for it."

"What if we don't want a self-cleaning crockpot?" Pirate Doug inquired as my small army nodded in agreement.

"Then you're an idiot," I shouted. "A self-cleaning crockpot ensures that your Johnson will be happy for years to come."

"Pun intended?" Del asked with a wide grin.

"I made a pun?" I asked, going back over my last sentence.

"Yep," Del said. "A bad one."

"Then yes," I said, taking a bow even though I still couldn't figure out my unintentional brilliance. "Pun intended. Boys, get ready to sprint. We're going in for the kill."

I was positive I heard moans and a few curses, but they would thank me later. I was sure of it.

3
NO SHIRT. NO SHOES. NO SERVICE

"ARE YOU KIDDING ME?" I SHOUTED AS I LANDED IN A PILE OF snow with a thud. "Do you people know who I am?"

It was the eighth store we'd been bodily removed from. We'd spent more time in the parking lot regrouping than we had shopping. My nuts were about to disappear. Snow in my diaper was not good for my package.

"What is wrong with these humans?" I roared as I shook the icy crystals off my body.

"No shirt. No Shoes. No Service," Bonar said, pointing at a sign on the front door of the establishment we'd just been thrown out of.

"That's nonsense," I snapped.

"Them thars the rules, yar Majesty," Upton informed me. "Would ye like me to go in and pilfer ye a shirt and shoes?"

The offer was lovely, but I hadn't covered my beautifully muscled chest in centuries. It was a sin to hide such perfection. However, self-cleaning crockpots were on the line here.

"Yes," I said. "I will take one for the team."

Again, I was sure I heard laughter from my men, but my balls were screaming. If it took a shirt and shoes to get some heat on my nuts, so be it.

"I shall pilfer my Pappy's clothing!" Pirate Doug announced as he took off at a clip into a store we'd not yet tried. "Be prepared to run for your lives!"

"Shite," I muttered. "The boy's an imbecile. My plans are falling apart."

Del grinned. "Not to mention, he just entered a clothing store for women."

"Double shite."

"You look fine," Cupid assured me, trying not to laugh and failing miserably.

If we hadn't traveled all the way to the frozen tundra arsehole of the United States, I would have called it a day and zapped the shite out of my disrespectful army. However, my Johnson's happiness was on the line. I was going to prevail.

"Pink really isn't my color," I said, glancing down at the cropped, hot-pink disaster of a shirt that Pirate Doug had stolen. The only saving grace was it was so tight that my pecs were clearly defined. The knee-high Santa socks barely came above my ankles and the low-heeled pumps were three sizes too small. However, I met the ridiculous requirements now.

"With your green hair, it's quite preppy," Keith pointed out unhelpfully.

"And yar hairy legs look fabulous in the heels," Bonar added... also unhelpfully.

"Thank you," I replied. A compliment was a compliment no matter how embarrassing. "If anyone takes a picture of me, I will send them on a field trip to Hades for a few months. Am I clear?"

My men nodded. No one made eye contact. I wanted to take that as a sign of respect, but I wasn't an idiot. I looked absurd. The damned self-cleaning crockpot had better be worth it.

"Alright, do not leave your cart unattended for even a second. Women wearing sweatpants and snow boots will attempt to steal your merchandise. If you need to take a whiz, do it now. There are plenty of parked cars to pee on," I advised. "If you drain your Johnson in the store, we'll lose valuable running time. You must sprint and knock people out of your way, or you won't get shite. Am I clear?"

"What about swearing?" Pirate Doug asked.

I almost belted him again, but he made a fine point.

"Keep it semi-PG. Getting arrested for lewd behavior is not on the schedule. We can do this, boys. I can feel the tingle in my frozen balls."

"So, we're basically rationalizing our insanity because we want self-cleaning crockpots to get laid?" Cupid inquired.

I had to think about that for thirty seconds. "Yes. Yes, we are! Follow me."

~

THE INSIDE OF HOLES DEPARTMENT STORE WAS A clusterhump. People were hunched over carts growling at each other. I spied several particularly barbaric females with self-cleaning crockpots in their metal baskets. They appeared to have eaten their young for breakfast and I was unsure if we should tangle with them.

"Upton. Bonar," I whispered. "Crawl after the two human females in the leggings. They have the goods."

"Aye," Bonar said, dropping to the floor. "Do ye mean the ones that ye can tell thar religion of by the unfortunate tightness of the stretchy breeches?"

"Aye," I replied, pulling the rest of the men behind a pyramid of fuzzy blankets with Christmas scenes on them. "Get the booty and run for your life."

"Are we doing the bunch of Brady layaway plan on the booty?" Upton inquired as he too dropped to the ground and began to slither through the aisles.

"No," I called after them. "Too dangerous. Just grab the shite and run like a Kraken is on your arse."

"Roger that," Upton said.

"So pilfering is back on the table?" Pirate Doug asked, wrapping himself in a snowman blanket.

"What are you doing?" Del asked his brother.

"Disguising myself," Pirate Doug replied, stealthily moving to a manikin, removing the wig and plopping the blond mass of curls onto his head.

"It's not a bad idea," Cupid said with a shrug, plucking stunning brown wig from a manikin and putting it on.

"There are probably security cameras in here. How do I look?"

"Like an arse," Pirate Doug said with a grin.

"Excellent," Cupid replied with a laugh as he wrapped himself in a purple blanket with Christmas trees on it.

"Fine," I said, grabbing a red pageboy wig and twisting my mossy green hair beneath it. "Grab a wig and blanket, and let's get to it. No time to waste."

"Are we just stealing self-cleaning crockpots?" Rick asked, settling on a jet-black mohawk and a white blanket with little angels on it.

"Nay," I said, choosing a green swath of fuzzy material with midgets wearing red hats with puffy white globules on the tips. "Toasters, vacuum cleaners, blenders, and digital bathroom scales are also on the list of items that will guarantee blow jobs."

"I'd like to go on record and say that a toaster will *not* get you a blow job," Del announced as he adjusted his hot pink curly wig in the mirror.

For a brief and unsettling moment, I wondered if I should fight my son for the pink wig. It did match my shirt...

"I'd say diamonds and jewels are more likely to end in a blow job," Cupid added.

These idiots knew nothing. I'd never gone to bed last night after the Thanksgiving shiteshow. Six hours on the interwebs had given me all the correct information. I'd also been able to diagnose myself with twelve human diseases, learned how to short-sheet Zeus' bed, stumbled across a warning never to put a sock in the toaster, unearthed how to tape my thumbs to my hands so I could experience what it felt like to be a dinosaur, found out that orange is the new black and that I was indeed several inches taller than Jason Momoa. The interwebs were a wonderful time suck, and wildly educational.

"Nope," I insisted. "A self-cleaning crockpot is the gift that will keep on giving."

"You're sure about that?" Keith asked, wearing a silver wig with curls that went down to his arse.

"Positive," I replied. "Absolutely positive. Now let's go find some fucking self-cleaning crockpots."

"WHAT IN THE NAME OF ZEUS' FLABBY ARSE IS HAPPENING?" I yelled as I watched my poor idiot son, Pirate Doug, get attacked by a posse of sadistic shoppers.

We'd split up to suss out the crockpots. Apparently, that was a grave mistake. Wally would have my arse in a sling if something happened to her baby boy. Of course, if the boy lost an appendage, it would grow back. He was a Vampyre/Pirate. It would be itchy, but the imbecile would live.

"He got the last one," Rick yelled above the roar of the crowd. "Pirate Doug got the last self-cleaning crockpot. All hell is breaking loose."

"Save him," I shouted, grabbing an electric frypan and shoving it into my diaper. "Fill your pockets while we commence with the rescue. I'm pretty sure this is our last stop."

"This is our first stop," Keith yelled as he made an outstanding dive and ripped a pop-up hotdog toaster from the hands of a banshee who was trying to beat Pirate Doug to a pulp with it.

"Toss it to me, boy," I yelled to Keith as I swiped a box of finger food party plates from an unsuspecting consumer. "I'll put the toaster in my pants."

"Remind me to never use that toaster," Cupid grunted as he jumped into the fray to save Pirate Doug and got beaned by a blender.

"Get the blender," I yelled to Cupid. "It's on the list."

"I'm on it," Cupid shouted as he ducked a cake pan shaped like a Johnson.

"What kind of place is this?" Upton screamed as he pilfered the schlong pan and raised high it in the air. "Should we take this?"

"Yes," I commanded. "It will be an excellent ice breaker at parties."

"Dick parties?" Del asked with an eye roll right before he got taken down with a soft pretzel maker/cheese warmer.

"Serve's you right, boy," I said as I yanked my Genie spawn to his feet and quickly put the pretzel maker into my diaper. "Don't be dissing the Johnson."

"Won't make that mistake again," he said with a laugh. "Gotta save my brother."

My heart swelled with pride as my two boys battled the angry, hissing mob alongside each other. I'd clearly done something right.

"We're losing ground," Bonar called out as he climbed a tower of male fragrances to get away from the fiendish females who were trying to pry the bacon bowl maker from his hands.

"I *told* you we were going to die," Cupid snapped as he was being choked by a gal who wanted the yogurt maker he'd been wily enough to pilfer.

"Cut our losses and run," I bellowed. "Grab as much as you can and haul ass out of here."

My boys worked like a well-oiled, battered and bloody machine. Made me proud.

"The drag queens are getting away," a particularly homicidal female human screeched.

"Drag queens?" Keith asked as we sprinted out of Holes Department store like Hades was on our heels. "I love a good drag show. I didn't see any drag queens."

"We're the drag queens, idiot," Del said as he snapped his fingers and summoned his magic carpet. "Everyone, hop on. NOW."

My boy didn't have to ask twice. The cold-blooded, vicious, leggings-wearing mob was closing in. I was unsure if we'd pilfered enough self-cleaning crockpots to get laid, but we'd stolen an outstanding variety.

However, the most important thing was that we got out alive. Not that any of us could die very easily, but those human females were sadistic.

Flying on a magic carpet in thirty below weather wasn't my idea of a good time, but getting decapitated would have really sucked.

"So, boys," I said with a grin as I searched my loaded diaper for a bottle of rum to celebrate. "Same time next year?"

The language was so appalling, I laughed so hard I almost fell off the carpet. Black Friday was somewhat like getting racked. Once you had vomited, cried, and iced your Johnson, it wasn't such a big deal. I was confident that my men would join me again next year.

However, we were not coming back to North Dakota. My nuts couldn't take it.

IS THAT A CHRISTMAS TREE, OR ARE YOU JUST HAPPY TO SEE ME?

MYSTICAL ISLE WAS TRULY MAGICAL—HOT SUN, COOL OCEAN breezes, and plenty of rum. Wally had been correct about spending the holidays here. I hadn't felt so Christmassy in centuries. All that was needed was a little sprucing up and I had an outstanding plan.

"So, my lovely ladies, I was thinking we could wrap all the palm trees on the island in twinkling lights," I told my favorite Mermaids as we walked along the sandy shore on the glorious sunny morning. "We'll wrap the bottom of the trees in pink lights and the leaves in white. It will be spectacular!"

"That's a very bad idea," Petunia said, rubbing her stomach.

The orange-haired Mermaid was the mate of my Genie son Del and was expecting my granddaughter in the next few weeks. Petunia was a wonderfully violent lass, and I was hoping they'd name the child after me. Poseidonia had such a nice ring to it.

"Petunia," I said carefully, placing my huge frame behind a pile of colorful beach chairs just in case she went for my balls. The gals were small but ferocious. "I realize the pregnancy hormones have made you unreasonably hungry, somewhat bulbous and more homicidal than usual, but I think you should have a little holiday spirit. Being a flinch isn't very Christmassy of you."

"Mmmkay, all of that was so wrong that if I didn't love you like an unrelated, inebriated father, I would have to kill you," Petunia said as her four Mermaid cousins nodded in agreement. "And what in the hell and seashells is a *flinch?*"

"Shite," I muttered, trying to remember the name Tallulah had supplied on the beach a few weeks ago. The hairy, green, ham-stealing bastard was making me look like an idiot.

Fourteen days post-battle, my men were still recovering from Black Friday. It had taken three days for my nuts to thaw out. I'd hidden all the booty in a shack on the beach and put a large sign on it. *Poseidon's Poop Shack* was sure to keep everyone away. The self-cleaning crockpots were safe. Sadly, we'd only been able to pilfer three crockpots, but the other items were outstanding. The hot dog toaster was a homerun. I'd be willing to forgo a self-cleaning crockpot for a machine that could perfectly char weenies and toast the buns at the same time.

"Would someone be so kind as to define flinch?" I inquired.

Ariel, the lovely blue-haired Mermaid, mated to the

brain-challenged Selkie, Keith, stepped forward. "A flinch is a reflex response to severe and sudden pain."

"Kind of like what you're going to experience if you keep talking," Madison the pink-haired beauty who was mated to Rick, the vegan Werewolf, told me with a raised brow and a laugh.

"Flinch isn't what I meant at all," I said, quickly backing away.

My Mermaid gals were wonderfully violent—a trait I both feared and adored.

"He means the Grinch," Tallulah informed the girls with an eye roll.

"Yes! Thank you. That could have taken hours and we need to get cracking on the trees," I informed the girls.

The gals squinted at me and I was sure they were trying not to laugh. I casually glanced down to make sure I was wearing my diaper. It would be terribly embarrassing to show my goods to the lasses I loved like daughters.

Thank the gods I was dressed.

"Who's going to explain it to him?" Misty the delightful green-haired Mermaid inquired. Misty was mated to the arsehole Cupid.

The five Mermaids looked like a lovely box of busty crayons. All Mermaids' hair and eyes were set from birth. Petunia's shade was orange. Madison's color was pink, Ariel's was blue, Misty's was emerald green and Tallulah's was lavender. Each Mermaid's hair and eyes were unique to them and no two were alike. However, the color of their tails changed with their moods and their fashion choices. It seemed to me that they always matched their tail—or when in human form, their sarong skirt—to their bikini tops.

"Explain what?" I asked.

"I'll do it," Tallulah said with a long sigh. "First let's talk about the shape of the trunk of a palm tree."

"Aye," I said somewhat confused but willing to play along.

"Can you describe it for me?" she inquired.

"Is this a game?" I asked perking up. I loved games, especially poker.

"Sure," Tallulah said with a laugh.

"Excellent! I shall play and I will win. The bottom of a palm tree is narrow and it widens to a nice wide curve at the top. Reminds me of a Johnson."

"Yep," Tallulah said, biting down on her lip. "And what's on top?"

I was thrilled I got the answer correct. My luck with *Jeopardy* was dreadful. Wally kicked my arse every time we played along with the TV show. I wished Wally was here now to hear my superb intelligence.

"On the top of a palm tree is a delightful spray of leaves fanning out and resembling a liquid explosion," I told the snickering group. My way with words was always a hit. Most of the time I didn't realize how funny I actually was. I was that good.

"Excellent," Tallulah said with a slight wince and a thumbs up.

Gods, this was a wonderful game—far better than poker.

"So if we wrap the trunks in pink lights and the leaves in

white lights… what do you think that would look like?" Tallulah asked.

Shite. The game just got tricky.

"Umm… can I have a hint?" I inquired. I'd gotten everything right thus far. I'd hate to fail on the bonus question.

"You compared the trunk of the tree to a man part. Right?" Tallulah asked.

Did I? Shite. I really shouldn't drink before 8 a.m. Wait. I did…

"A salami," I bellowed with relief. "The trunk of a palm tree resembles a rod of love."

"Mmmkay," Tallulah said, gagging a little. "Let's get to the root of the problem here."

"Ewwwww," Ariel said with a laugh. "Icky pun, dudette."

Tallulah smacked herself in the forehead and groaned. "My bad. Totally unintentional."

I had no clue what the hell they were talking about, but I laughed along with my girls.

"Hilarious," I shouted, slapping my knee and forcing out uproarious laughter.

"He didn't get it," Misty said with a giggle.

"Not even a little bit," Petunia said grinning.

"Get what?" I asked.

"If we wrap the trunks of the palm trees in pink twinkle lights and the leaves in white, it might look a bit phallic," Tallulah explained.

I pulled a bottle of rum from my diaper and took a long swig. It gave me time to think. What in the Seven Seas did *phallic* mean?

"I don't see the problem," I told the girls, hoping that was the winning answer.

The Mermaids rolled their eyes in unison so hard I was certain they'd gotten stuck in the backs of their heads.

"Let me try," Madison said, patting her sister on the back. "We run a resort. We have human guests. Right?"

"Yes," I said. Thank gods the questions had gotten easier.

"How do you think our business would fare if we had an island covered in flashing, exploding wankers?"

Shite. Another complicated question. I'd go vague on my answer and hope it was correct.

"Still not seeing a problem here," I replied, opening a few of the beach chairs to make a barricade just in case they decided to attack.

"For the love of everything sandy," Petunia chimed in with a grunt of laughter. "Poseidon, if we light the trunks of the trees in pink, they'll look more like Johnsons than they already do. If we light the leaves in white it will appear the Johnsons are *active*. You feel me?"

"I see," I said, nodding sagely. "And this is a problem?"

"YES," they shouted in unison.

"You're sure about that?" I tried again.

"YES," my gals repeated.

"Okaaaaay," I said, devising a new plan. "The flashing, exploding, active Johnsons are out. I find that a bit sad, but I understand that glowing salamis mid-orgasm might not be good for business."

"Umm... thank you," Tallulah said, shaking her head and groaning.

"Not to worry, I have another outstanding idea," I announced rubbing my hands together with glee.

"Hang on a sec," Misty said, snapping her fingers and producing four alcoholic pina coladas and one virgin pina colada for the pregnant Petunia. "It's five o'clock somewhere, ladies."

"Correct," Tallulah said, taking the frothy drink and downing it. "Okay. Now I'm good to hear Poseidon's next idea."

I wasn't sure if I should be insulted or proud. I chose proud.

Madison, Ariel and Petunia followed suit and finished off their drinks in one swallow.

"After learning he named his online dating service *Immortal Snatch*, I live in abject fear of the God of the Sea's plans," Ariel said with a giggle.

"As well you should," I said with pride, raising my bottle of rum high in a toast. It was good to strike a little fear in my subjects. It kept their respect level for me quite high.

"The idea?" Madison asked with a grin.

"Yes, yes, yes," I said. "The human creatures enjoy a little something Christmassy called Guelph on Oneself."

"I'm sorry. *What?*" Misty asked, magically whipping up another round of drinks. "It sounds gross."

"And messy," Ariel said.

"And potentially smelly," Misty added.

"You must know what I'm talking about," I insisted, taking the pina colada that was offered. I usually preferred my rum straight from the bottle I kept in my diaper, but I never turned down a libation. "The little bastard hides in underwear drawers—scares the hell out of everyone with his glassy eyes and psychotic smile."

"Umm… no clue," Ariel said, squinting at me.

"Dresses in red—no discernable schlong even though his pants are ridiculously tight," I tried again. "He poops peppermints according to the pictures on the interwebs."

"How drunk are you?" Madison asked with a giggle.

"Elf on a Shelf?" Tallulah asked with an eye roll. "Do you mean Elf on a Shelf?"

"Yes," I bellowed with joy. Names were a real bitch to remember. I was hard-pressed to remember my nine hundred and whatever children's names. I couldn't be expected to remember the name of a tiny, perverted eunuch in a red hat. "However, I have come up with a twist on it."

"Do we dare ask?" Misty inquired.

"Won't matter," Petunia said. "He's gonna tell us anyway."

"Right you are," I announced grandly. "I have already procured the species that we need. I have placed all of them in the small pool in the back of the resort."

The Mermaid's eyes grew wide with what I could only assume as awe… or terror. I was sticking with awe.

"We will put Mackerels on the Mermaids, Puffers on the Pirates, Clams on that bastard Cupid, a Sea Cucumber on Keith the Selkie, a Walrus on Rick the Werewolf and a Giant Squid on Del the Genie. It's genius!" I said taking a bow… to silence… and then gasps of horror.

What was wrong here? There were absolutely no flashing active Johnsons involved.

"We don't have a small pool," Tallulah whispered, paling.

"Of course, you do," I replied. "Right next to the big pool."

"Umm… that's a hot tub," Misty said as she dropped her drink and began to run back to the resort. "A really *hot* tub."

"Shite," I bellowed as I joined the posse of shapely sprinting crayons. Had I turned a wonderful Christmassy idea into seafood chowder? There would not be enough rum on the island if I'd harmed the little swimming bastards.

"THEY'RE ALL GOING TO LIVE," WALLY SAID, GIVING ME A HUG as I blubbered like a baby next to the hot tub.

"Ohhh, Wally," I said, shaking my head in shame. "Those clams were looking a little rubbery. Are you sure they made it?"

"They made it. They had a few unflattering things to say about you, but they'll be fine. Everyone is happily back in the ocean," she assured me with a smile. "You're a colossal jackass, but your heart is in the right place, my lover."

"It was awful," I whispered. "And the smell—not very Christmassy at all."

Wally snapped her slim lovely fingers and produced a fine bottle of rum. After taking a ladylike sip, she handed the bottle over. My gal was perfect.

"Darling, do you think you might be trying a wee bit too hard?" she inquired, re-pinning the side of my diaper that had come loose when I'd given the Walrus mouth to mouth resuscitation. The fat bastard really needed to brush his teeth, but he didn't deserve to be boiled alive for bad breath.

"No clue what you're talking about," I said, taking a healthy pull on the bottle.

"The real meaning of Christmas isn't about the stuff. It's about family and love."

"And self-cleaning crockpots," I added and then smacked myself in the head with the now empty bottle.

Wally's eyes lit up like a Christmas tree. "Is that a real thing?"

"Darn tootin' it is," I told her. "My frozen nuts can attest to it."

"And am I getting one for Christmas?" she purred as she ran her finger seductively down my chest.

"Aye," I choked out, realizing I would electrocute the shite out of my own kin so Wally would have one of the three self-cleaning crockpots we'd absconded with. I had my sex-life to consider. My jolly roger won out over common sense daily where my mate was concerned. Not to mention, I'd worn low-heeled pumps for the damned appliances. I deserved first pick. And the boys would be fine with a zap of lightning or two.

"Well," she said with a shudder of delight. "As arousing as a self-cleaning crockpot is, I still think you might have gone overboard."

"Nay," I assured the love of my immortal life. "I'm just getting started. It will be outstanding because I'm the greatest god of all of those whiney shites on Mount Olympus."

"I'm quite sure Zeus would disagree," Wally said with a laugh.

"Well then, Zeus can kiss my diapered arse. I will produce a Christmas no one will ever forget."

I was fairly sure I heard a chorus of moans come from the resort, but I was so busy kissing my she-devil, I must have imagined it.

5

THE KRAKEN WHO STOLE CHRISTMAS

"So all I have to do is tell the wee ones a Christmas story?" Pirate Doug asked, modeling his new red breeches and puffy green shirt.

"Aye," I replied, closing my eyes so I wouldn't punch my boy in the head. His fashion sense was appalling. There was more material in his shirt than forty of my diapers.

"I don't know any Christmas stories," Pirate Doug said as he rotated to examine himself at every angle in the mirror of his quarters. "Do these breeches make my arse look fat?"

"Nay," Upton said, reassuring my dolt of a son. "Ye look like a right thunderin' worm- riddled fish gizzard. Yar arse is quite fetchin' in yar breeches."

"Really? Do you think so?" Pirate Doug asked, still worried.

"Aye," Bonar added. "The balance of yar puffy shirt with the breeches is just right. Ye resemble an eyeliner wearin' dingey dangler. Makes me proud to be on yar crew, Captain."

They were all idiots.

"Outstanding," Pirate Doug bellowed as he checked his backside one last time.

"Are we done?" I inquired, pulling a bottle of liquid encouragement from my diaper. "Can we get back to Christmas here?"

"Aye," my son said, taking a seat on the chair opposite me. "Do you have a particular story in mind, Pappy?"

"Nay," I replied. "Although the one about the scrinch is a popular one."

"The who?" Pirate Doug asked, confused.

"Never mind," I muttered. I seriously needed to give up on that hairy green fucker.

"I know a couple of Christmassy tales," Upton volunteered.

"Aye, me too," Bonar added.

While wary of the Pirates' version of a holiday yarn, I was greatly relieved. It would take me a damned week to remember the name of the green ham-stealer. However, Upton was double-jointed and could lick his own nards. The thought of a Christmas spiel coming from him was slightly alarming, but beggars couldn't be choosers. A Christmas story for the children was necessary for the holiday to be perfect.

"Excellent," I said, standing up to leave. I was on the verge of telling my imbecile son that his arse looked large in his breeches just to see him implode. That would be fun but counterproductive. I needed his outstanding showmanship with the wee ones. "We will have Christmas storytime at two o'clock sharp on the beach. I will let the humans know!"

"Will yar be servin' alcohol?" Upton inquired.

The scrawny Pirate asked a legitimate question. I had to think about that for thirty-two seconds.

"Humans are a tricky bunch," I said as I paced the room in deep thought. "Not sure what the drinking rules are for bairns under the age of eight. Does anyone know?"

"Nay," Bonar said. "Methinks it's a fine idea though. The little scallywags should enjoy the holiday too."

"And methinks we'd be greasy-haired rope burns if we didn't provide the wee landlubbers with a fine time."

The idiots made an excellent point. Something felt incredibly wrong here, but I'd go with the flow on this one.

"Done. We will be serving rum to the children," I announced. "No one will say we didn't provide an epic outing."

"You're a dumbass," Wally hissed as she zapped me with a bolt of lightning that made me randy and would most definitely leave a scar. "You *never* serve children alcohol. Am I clear?"

The Mermaids ran around the beach taking the bottles of rum from the wee ones as the human parents looked on in shock. One little mistake and everyone freaked out. What had the Universe come to?

"Aye," I said, rubbing my backside. "My bad. We just wanted the children to have a little fun."

Wally's eye roll deserved an Academy Award. I placed myself behind a sandcastle just in case she felt the need to electrocute me again.

"It's illegal and only an idiot would come up with such a ridiculous plan," she snapped.

"Your point?" I asked, confused.

Wally's eyes narrowed to slits. It took all my well-endowed mate had not to rip me a new arsehole. It was a fine thing that there were semi-inebriated kidlets around at the moment.

"The girls have enough lawsuits to contend with due to Upton licking his marbles in public. They do not need to add intoxication of minors to the list. You feel me, Poseidon?" Wally growled.

"I'd love to, but there are people around," I replied. "Maybe if you came behind the sandcastle with me, I could cop a quick feel of your tremendous knockers."

The bolt of lightning from my lover came fast and singed my diaper right off my arse. Thankfully, I always carried a spare for situations just like this one. Quickly covering my enormous Johnson, I sprinted away from my pissed off she-devil. We still had storytime ahead of us. And I was fairly sure if I was engulfed in flames it wouldn't be very Christmassy.

"Pirate Doug," I shouted, ducking behind a bush as Wally advanced. "Begin the Christmas yarn. NOW!"

"I'm on it," my son yelled back, gathering the tiny humans into a circle.

Upton and Bonar flanked him. They were a motley trio. There was enough material in their puffy shirts to cover the island, but they were all clad in red and green. I appreciated the holiday effort even though they looked like arses.

"Alright, ye bandana wearin' platoon splinters," Upton bellowed to the confused faces of everyone. "It's time for the Christmas yarn. Ye need to sit yar cutlass flappin' bilge drinkin' arses down and listen to me Captain or ye will walk the plank."

"Did he just threaten the children?" I heard one human mother inquire.

"Nay," I assured her from behind my bush. "Tis Pirate speak for *enjoy the show*."

The woman thanked me for the explanation and then scurried away in horror. Looking down, I realized I'd forgotten to pin my diaper. No worries. A glimpse of a god Johnson was a rare and precious gift.

Heaving in a huge breath, Pirate Doug turned to his crew and once again inquired if his arse looked bulbous in his breeches. After many assurances that his backside was wonderful, he went for it.

"T'was the night before Christmas, when all over the beach... Not a cod-faced tar stain was stirring, not even a leach!" Pirate Doug shouted in his outdoor voice.

It was a fine start. I was proud of my boy. The children laughed. I was unsure if it was the tiny bit of rum they'd ingested or the zest with which my idiot son told his tale. It mattered not. We were creating a fine tradition here.

"The weevil-eating seashells were hung by the palm tree with care, in hopes that the bloodthirsty Christmas Kraken would soon grow some nard hair," Pirate Doug went on, clearly getting into it.

I was riveted and wondered where the fabulous story would go. It was an excellent beginning.

"What in the hell and seashells did he just say?" Tallulah demanded as we all now stood on the outskirts of the circle and listened to the tale.

"Pretty sure he said he wants the Kraken to grow pubes," Petunia said, trying not to laugh.

"That's exactly what he said," Misty confirmed, shaking her head. "I can feel the lawsuits coming."

"It might get better," Ariel said, being the ever-hopeful Mermaid that she was.

"Or worse," Madison said.

"My son is an imbecile," Wally snapped. "Be prepared to electrocute him if this continues to go downhill. He'll live."

"Good plan," Tallulah whispered.

I felt like the gals were being a little harsh, but what did I know? I thought getting the small humans soused was an excellent idea. Keeping my trap shut, I listened and hoped to the Seven Seas and back that Pirate Doug would not wax poetic about his schlong. That was surefire electrocution material.

"The children all wrestled—now bloodied and bruised," Pirate Doug shouted as Bonar and Upton began to pantomime the story much to the children's and my delight.

The right hook from Upton that most likely broke Bonar's nose was inspired. The blood spurted everywhere.

Pirate Doug kept going like a pro even though he was now covered in blood. "I repeat," he yelled. "The children all wrestled—now bloodied and bruised, while their parents all wished they'd left the little fuckers at home and went on a cruise! And Mamma in her thong and I in my fabulous puffy shirt had just settled down for a hump and a squirt."

"Did he say *fuckers?*" Tallulah asked, paling.

"And *thong?*" Madison added with a groan.

"And a *hump and a squirt?*" Misty choked out.

"Aye," I said, hushing the gals. "It's getting good."

The punch in the head from Wally came from left field. I felt it was quite unfair. I was simply supporting our idiot son. Hopping back up, I moved away from the judgmental women. Clearly, they had no Christmas spirit.

The crowd was with Pirate Doug if all the gasping was anything to go by. He continued with gusto that brought a tear of pride to my eye.

"When out on the fake-bearded, crab-infested sand there arose such a ruckus, I jumped off my purple swimming hooker to see what in the peg-legged, salty nards was causing the itch in my tuckus," Pirate Doug said, gaining more confidence as the children began to cry with joy at such a worthy tale. "I tripped over the handcuffs and vibrators and fell on my arse with a crash. Ran out of the wrong door and in the pool made a splash."

The rhyming was outstanding. I clapped and whistled and then ducked a bolt of lightning from Wally that came within an inch of decapitating me.

"I cussed like a sailor," Pirate Doug said as Bonar and Upton let loose with a string of curses that proved they'd spent most of their lives on the sea. It was quite educational.

"I repeat!" Pirate Doug shouted over the disgusting words leaving his men's mouths. "I cussed like a sailor and stubbed my big toe. I was sure that bastard Man on the

Moon flipped me off, so I yanked down my pants and gave that glowing arsehole a show."

Bonar and Upton mooned the crowd. Human parents began to grab their spawns and run like hell. The ghostly white arses of the Pirates were a bit much, but it was part of the story. I found it brave, creative and horrifying that they were so committed.

"When what to my wondering eyes should appear," Pirate Doug kept going, oblivious to the shiteshow he was creating. "But a fat bastard Kraken, holding a beer!"

"That's it," Tallulah shouted.

"Electrocute. NOW," Wally roared.

It was horrible… yet very colorful. The red breeches and puffy green shirts were quite Christmassy as they blew up in flames. Thankfully, only three lawsuits were filed. The Pirates healed up quite nicely after a few hours and we were all made to sleep on the beach as punishment.

All in all, I'd say that storytime was a great success.

6

WAIT. WE FORGOT ABOUT HANUKKAH

"DOES ANYONE HERE HAPPEN TO BE JEWISH?" I ASKED AS I made my way through the buffet line at the afternoon Holiday Tiki Party.

"Is that a new fashion?" Pirate Doug inquired only to be whacked on the back of the head by his mother.

"Dumbass," Wally muttered as she continued down the lunch buffet line as if she hadn't just sent her only son flying into the salad.

Pirate Doug landed with a thud in a mound of seaweed salad. Everyone ignored it. It was par for the course. Tallulah and her sisters had decided that we were not allowed around the human guests anymore as the lawsuits kept rolling in. Our buffet was on the private side of the resort. I quite enjoyed being with family only. However, that meant the gals were free to electrocute us more freely as well. No pain, no gain as I always liked to say.

"Nay, not a fashion," I replied to my idiot spawn as he

removed seaweed from his hair. "I believe it's a club. They have an extra-long Christmas according to the interwebs."

"Nope," Tallulah said with an eye roll as she set a platter of bizarre-looking vegan delicacies on the table for Rick and Madison. "It's a human religion and they do not celebrate Christmas."

"But they *do* have presents," I volunteered. "*Eight days* of presents which is outstanding. I was thinking we could join their club and..."

"Nope," Wally said cutting me off.

"But it would be..." I tried again.

"No can do, Poseidon," Petunia said. "It's a stretch that we're even celebrating Christmas. We worship a whole bunch of idiot gods—*like you*—not the God celebrated at Christmas."

"I think you are all being clinches," I announced, ignoring the insult and focusing on the *worship of me* part of Petunia's statement. "Presents are the best part of the holiday."

"Not happening—and it's Grinch, not clinch," Tallulah informed me. "It's not a club and it's disrespectful to join a human religion to get presents."

"Are you sure?" I questioned.

"YES!" all the females shouted.

The males were simply confused. Again, par for the course. However, at the risk of mass electrocution that I didn't think my arse could handle, I dropped the subject. I had a better plan anyway.

"Attention ladies, gentlemen, and Pirate Doug. At sunset today, we will be doing a family Christmas portrait on the beach," I announced to a very un-Christmassy round of moans and groans. "I have procured Christmas sweaters for all to wear. You will find the stolen goods in your rooms. We are including some of the extended family as well. I've invited Bony Velma Dustface, my stanky Sea Hag daughter, to be in the photograph. I have supplied nose plugs as well. You will notice they are green in the spirit of Christmas. You will each find a pair laid out for you with your sweater. Simply shove one up each nostril and we will all live through Bony Velma's putrid aroma."

"Won't that look like we're all sporting boogers?" Keith asked, with his hand raised politely.

While I appreciated his manners, I wasn't fond of the backtalk. Quickly, blasting him with a non-lethal lightning bolt, I ignored him. Boogers were *not* made of plastic. He was being ridiculous.

"We will meet at 7 p.m. on the beach. Do not be late."

I had wonderful plans to rub my perfect Christmas in the noses of the other gods. Zeus would be wildly jealous. It was turning out to be an outstanding day.

"I WILL *NOT* WEAR THIS," WALLY SAID, PACING THE LIVING room of our grand suite in agitation.

"You have to, my love," I replied. "Everyone shall be sporting a Christmas sweater. It will be a beautiful moment caught in history and Zeus will shite his toga with envy."

"Does *this* look beautiful to you?" Wally griped, modeling her holiday wear.

Son of a sea biscuit. I should have looked at the damned sweaters before I'd pilfered them. In my defense, the store was closed and dark when I'd robbed it. Not to mention, I was wasted.

Wally wore a lime green sweater with sparkly red garland circles surrounding each of her tremendous bosoms. There was a strategically placed jingle ball in the center of each garland circle. I found it strangely arousing, but could also see her point.

It wasn't something she would normally wear. Actually, it was something she would never wear, but there wasn't time to dash off to Florida to steal a less heinous garment.

"You are beautiful no matter what you wear," I said, ready to run like Hades was on my arse if necessary.

Wally grew quiet. This was always a very bad sign. It normally ended in an inferno of sorts.

"If I agree to wear this pornographic disaster, I get control of the TV remote for six months," she said.

Shite. I was going to be stuck watching chick flicks and cooking shows for half a year.

Closing my eyes, I sighed. The loss of Chuck Norris movies was a small price to pay to keep my arse from being set on fire.

"Deal," I told my love.

"And I get to drive the Hummer," she added with an evil little grin.

Double shite. Wally drove like an old, blind human woman. My mate had already crashed fifteen of my Hummer fleet while doing her makeup in the side-view mirror as she drove. I only had one left. Decisions sucked...

but a family Christmas picture would make Zeus green with envy.

"Deal," I choked out on a whisper.

"I can't hear you, darling," she replied with a raised brow as she made to remove the sweater.

"Deal," I shouted. "Let's do this before I lose my shirt."

"You don't wear a shirt," Wally said with a giggle.

She made a fine point, but I would make an exception this fine evening for an epic family holiday photo.

INWARDLY, I CURSED MYSELF FOR BEING PLASTERED WHEN I'D pilfered the Christmas wear from the Snuggly Sweater Showroom. Although, the colors were truly spectacular. By the disgruntled expressions of my nearest and dearest, I wasn't sure we would get the outstanding photo I was hoping for.

At least the sunset was gorgeous—fiery red and pink in the sky. It was a fitting backdrop for an epic family portrait. My Clam band had arrived and was strumming delightful Christmas polka music. My musical boys were slightly odoriferous, human-sized clams with arms and legs and no discernible faces. The boys had no social skills to speak of, but they played a mean polka.

"Are you serious?" Tallulah demanded as she marched out onto the beach, pointing at her sweater. "You expect me to wear this?"

"I'm good with mine. Although, the Johnson could have

been a bit larger in my opinion," Pirate Doug announced, modeling his pea-green woolen pullover.

Tallulah punched him in the head. "Doug's sweater says *Snowballs Deep* on it and the freaking snowman has a fuzzy blue Johnson and nards for the love of everything disgusting," she griped. "And I'm wearing a Christmas tree that says *I Don't Want Your Balls On Me.*"

"I see no problem here," I said, beginning to sweat.

The sweaters were bad. I actually agreed with my irate Mermaid daughter-in-law. I could only hope that the rest weren't quite as heinous.

"What in the hell and seashells were you drinking when you picked these out?" Petunia shouted as she and my son Del stomped out onto the beach. "Is there a reason you gave *Santa is a Fat Bastard* to the pregnant Mermaid? Are you trying to tell me something?"

"Nay," I said, pulling a bottle of rum from my diaper and downing the contents. At this point, I realized the drunker the better.

"Pappy," Del said with an eye roll. "A gingerbread man with a beer bong isn't exactly *Christmassy.*"

Wally laughed and flipped me off. I was pretty sure I had very few allies right now.

Next to arrive were Ariel and Keith. The glare on Ariel's face was reason enough to partake in a second bottle of rum.

"You're going to owe me," Ariel grumbled, wearing a jumper that said *Merry Christmas You Filthy Animal.*

"I like mine. A fat, naked, bearded man on a Unicorn is cool," Keith announced only to be zapped with a sparkling, blue bolt of magic by his mate.

So far, I had the two most idiotic of my men on my side. Pirate Doug and Keith weren't the sharpest tools in the shed, but I was delighted to have at least a little support.

Misty and Cupid and Baby Thornycraft—the little Pirate they were raising—entered the scene. If looks could kill, I'd be walking the plank.

"I should tie your nuts in a knot," Misty snapped, wearing a hot pink sweater that said *Frosty the Blowman* on it that pictured a snowman on his knees pleasuring Santa.

That one threw me for a loop. I hadn't realized that Santa swung both ways. And who knew snowmen had knees? Thankfully, Baby Thornycraft's sweater only had a reindeer taking a dump on it.

"You've lost your mind, old man," Cupid said with a laugh. "This will certainly go down in history as a day no one will forget."

Cupid's sweater was a blinding, bright red that said *I've Got Ho-Ho-Ho's in Different Area Codes.* Definitely non-traditional. If I had any fashion sense, I would say it was hideous. It was excellent that I had no taste.

The next irate couple to grace the beach was Madison and Rick. I seriously hoped Madison wasn't carrying concealed weapons. The Mermaid had outstanding aim and her weapon of choice was a dagger. On the outside chance I was going to lose a nard, I hid behind the Clam Band.

"I'm standing in the back," Madison snapped, pointing at her sweater. "*Get Lit?*" she yelled. "Seriously? A freaking drunk Christmas tree telling everyone to get wasted?"

"Duuuude," Rick said shaking his head and chuckling. "I

would like to go on record for all to hear. I did not bang Santa no matter what this ugly sweater says."

"It says you *shagged* Santa, not *banged* Santa," Pirate Doug pointed out only to be tackled by all of his brothers-in-law at the same time.

"Boys," I bellowed. "Do not get blood on your sweaters. It will ruin the photo."

Wally slapped me up the backside of my head. "Blood will only help," she informed me.

With the violent brawl in full swing, we were joined by the rest of the family. Upton arrived with his mate, Yolanda the Yeti. Thankfully, their sweaters were only semi-offensive. Upton's sweater had Santa smoking a cigarette on it—or a joint. Yolanda's was covered in tiny midgets wearing red hats and dancing with each other... or possibly fornicating. I didn't have the time for Yolanda to go all Squatch on me, so I was delighted and relieved they seemed calm.

Bonar arrived with his mate, my great-great-great-great granddaughter and then some, Kim. With them was her adorable half-gnome—half-god, toddler son Neville. Upton, Kim and Neville were clad in sweaters that said *Happy New Year 2001* on them.

No wonder they were only fifty cents—not that I'd paid for any of them.

"As soon as Bony Velma arrives, we will take the photo," I announced.

"Can we make a bonfire and burn the sweaters when we're done?" Petunia inquired.

"Aye," I answered to cheers from the ungrateful crowd.

The disrespect was appalling, but I figured we could make s'mores over the woolen fire.

"What is that *smell?*" Cupid inquired, wrinkling his nose and gagging.

"Shite," I shouted. "Shove the plugs in your noses. I scent Bony Velma coming in fast. She's about three miles out."

"Oh my gods," Petunia choked out. "That's from *three miles* away?"

"Aye," Upton said, shoving the green plastic into his nostrils. "Bony Velma is a fine lass, but her aroma is like a pig-perfumed milkmaid."

"Or a cutlass flappin' fish stink," Bonar added.

"Aye, good one," Upton agreed with a nod. "But methinks that pegged legged salty nards of a sea rat might be a wee bit more accurate."

"While ye make a fine point," Bonar said, helping little Neville insert the plugs. "Methinks a thunderin' bilge rat embedded in a crab-infested dingy-dangler really nails the aroma."

I agreed with every word the Pirates said even though I didn't understand much of it.

"I'm here," Bony Velma announced as she landed on the beach in a cloud of putrid green smoke. "Great sweaters! Do you have one for me, Pappy?"

Shite. I'd forgotten about my odoriferous spawn. I felt horrible. I wasn't too fond of Velma due to her trying to kill me for a few centuries, but I was trying to be a better father now. The smelly hag had promised not to attempt any more waterborne assassinations and I had made a vow not to mention her hygiene or excessive body hair in public.

So far so good. However, everything could so south fast. A fit from Bony Velma could blow Mystical Isle off the map.

"Darling," Wally said, giving me a pointed look and then going to greet Velma. "You don't need one! The green haze that follows you like a noxious, pungent rash is far better than a hideous sweater."

"Are you sure?" Velma asked as her eyes narrowed dangerously.

"Positive," Wally gushed to a slightly happier Bony Velma.

"I love you," I whispered to Wally as I warily watched Velma think through what my mate had just said.

"You have to do the dishes for a year," Wally informed me under her breath.

"Shite," I muttered.

"And you have to take me to a Celine Deon concert and six Disney on Ice programs *and* not bitch," she added.

"Is that all?" I hissed with an eye roll.

"Nope," she replied with a grin. "You will come to Couples Jazzercize with me every Tuesday for the next year and you will wear shorts over your diaper so you don't expose your nards."

"But my nards are outstanding," I countered, hoping to win at least part of the negotiation.

Wally simply raised a brow and threateningly wiggled her pinky finger. It made my roger very jolly—too jolly. My Johnson was a bastard. He'd betrayed me yet again. With all the blood in my pecker, I couldn't even recall what blackmail Wally had insisted upon, so I nodded my head in agreement.

"Aye," I whispered. "We have a deal."

"Do you have any clue what I just asked?" Wally inquired, glancing down at my tented diaper with a grin.

"Nay," I told her with a laugh. "But if it makes you happy, I'll do it."

Wally's laugh was what I lived for and she didn't disappoint. Shoving me farther behind my blind Clams until my Johnson wound down, she continued to have my back.

"I'll tell you what, Velma," Wally said. "After the photo, you can have all of the sweaters and hold a party with the Sea Hags in your cave. What we truly need for a perfect holiday picture is your gamy fumes to give the photo a dreamy and fetid effect."

"Really?" Bony Velma asked shyly.

"Really," Wally announced as she carefully hugged Velma without upchucking.

My gal was my hero.

"Okay," Tallulah grunted as she and her sisters broke up the brawl. "Let's get this shit over with. My sweater is itchy. Where's the photographer?"

Mother humpin' shite monsters. I knew there was something I'd forgotten.

"Umm… the Clams," I shouted, grabbing the closest faceless mollusk by the scruff of his neck and holding him high above my head. "Clarence shall capture the precious Christmassy moment in time."

"He has no face," Pirate Doug pointed out rather unhelpfully.

"Which means he's blind," Keith added.

So much for having the two most idiotic men on my side.

Tallulah laughed and pulled on her purple locks. "You forgot to hire a photographer?"

Sighing and letting my head fall to my chest, I began to sniffle. "Aye," I blubbered. "I did indeed."

"Not a problem, Pappy," Bony Velma announced producing a long stick with a clothespin attached to the end of it. "I have a selfie stick!"

"What's a selfie stick?" I asked.

"You clip a phone to it and we take the picture ourselves," she replied.

"Outstanding!" I bellowed. "I have now decided that I genuinely like you, Velma."

"Really?" she squealed with delight.

"She pulled that selfie stick out of her arse. Literally," Pirate Doug whispered in my ear.

Holding back my bile took great effort. "Umm… mostly. I mostly like you," I told my rank daughter. "Everyone bunch in together. Quickly, before anyone heaves. Bony Velma will take the picture. NO ONE touch the selfie stick. It belongs to Velma and I have heard a rumor that it has possibly been residing in her arse. Am I clear?"

The gasps and gags were audible, but thankfully Velma didn't notice. She was so excited to be in charge it was almost endearing—in a musty, malodorous way.

"Everyone is sick?" Velma inquired as she clipped her cellphone to the stick and raised it high.

"No," I said. "Why would you think that?"

"All the green boogers in everyone's noses," she replied.

"Told you," Keith said with a laugh as I blasted him with a bolt of lightning.

"Yes, well, it is cold and flu season," I lied as I picked up the passed-out Keith and threw him over my shoulder.

"We're gonna have to do it in sections," Velma announced.

"Unacceptable," I shouted. "We must all be in the picture together."

"No can do," the Sea Hag shot back.

"Just hurry up," Petunia begged. "It's awfully funky-reeky right now and I'm not sure how much longer the boogers will hold up. You feel me, Poseidon?"

"Aye," I said, feeling a little light-headed myself. "I shall simply glue the pieces of the picture together. Problem solved! We will still have our epic Christmas photo. Everyone smile. NOW."

The picture was horrifying. The boys were bleeding and their pilfered sweaters were torn. I'd forgotten to remove Keith from my shoulder and his arse was front and center. Tallulah and Madison were flipping the camera off and Upton and Bonar had decided that the picture needed a moon—two to be precise. At least their white and somewhat hairy arses would be easy to remove as the two idiot Pirates were on the far-left side.

Wally was laughing like a loon and half of the crew had their eyes closed. Little Neville and Baby Thornycraft, clearly uncomfortable with the plastic in their tiny nostrils, appeared to be picking their noses in the photo.

And the rest of us? We all looked like we were indeed

sporting green boogers. Well, all except Bony Velma who was holding the stick that she'd pulled out of her arse.

Whatever. After I'd glued the pieces together, I'd simply borrow some of Neville's crayons and fix everyone up. I could even draw some fucking breeches onto Upton and Bonar and make the boogers a lovely peach color.

All in all, I believe it turned out excellently.

No one died.

I'd call that a Christmas miracle.

7

DEAR SANTA, I'VE BEEN A VERY GOOD BOY...

"Shut your pieholes, gentlemen and Pirate Doug. I have incredibly insane news. Everyone must keep it on the down low. I don't want this getting out to too many people. It could adversely affect us," I said, glancing around to make sure we were alone.

The moon sat high and majestic in the sky and the stars twinkled, casting a shimmering glow on the ocean. The only sounds to be heard were the waves lapping at the shore... and the bitching of my men.

"Is the island going to be attacked?" Rick asked with concern as his tired eyes popped open in alarm.

"Nay, nay, nay," I said with a chuckle. "It has come to my attention that there may indeed be a Santa Claus. I just need to know if all of you have been good boys or bad boys this year. Apparently, Santa keeps some kind of bullshite list."

"Doesn't stealing electrical appliances put all of us on the bad boy list?" Keith asked.

"Absolutely not," I huffed, hoping like hell that wasn't true. "Those vicious human women in obscenely tight, stretchy breeches tried to kill us. We did what was necessary to get the fucking self-cleaning crockpots and live through it. Besides, we weren't pilfering for ourselves. We were illegally procuring items for others so it doesn't count."

"You also stole the Johnson and knocker Christmas sweaters," Pirate Doug pointed out.

"Had to," I said. "The store was closed."

"Sounds reasonable to me," my dolt of a son replied.

"Wait. You woke all of us up in the middle of the damned night and dragged us bodily onto the beach to tell us you believe in Santa Claus?" Cupid growled as he flopped down on a beach lounge and put a towel over his face.

"Where did you find the proof?" Keith asked with a huge yawn.

Of course, it *was* three in the morning and I *had* yanked my men from their slumber with their mates. However, I was sure there would be far more excitement about the wonderful news than I was observing.

"The almighty interwebs," I explained. "I even have an address!"

"Shall we TP Santa's yard?" Pirate Doug inquired. "I keep a fair amount of arse paper on the ship for cases like this."

"No, you idiot," I snapped. "We're going to send him a letter."

"Are you drunk?" Pirate Doug inquired, squinting at me.

"Don't ask ridiculous questions," I told him. Of course I am."

"And why are we going to send Santa a letter, Pappy?" Del asked, shoving Cupid off the lounge and taking it for himself.

"To get more presents," I said.

"Umm… call me crazy, but… " Rick began.

"Crazy Butt," I replied.

"Not what I meant," Rick said.

"But you *asked* me to call you Crazy Butt," I told him, confused.

"Nope. I didn't," Rick said with an eye roll.

"You did," I shot back with a bigger eye roll.

"Nope."

"Yep," I said.

"This could take all night and I really want to sleep in a bed with Misty," Cupid griped. "Let Rick get a damned sentence out, old man."

"As I was saying," Rick continued with a chuckle. "I think you might be putting a little too much emphasis on the material side of Christmas."

"Nonsense," I bellowed. "I'm not giving anyone *clothing* for Christmas. I don't know what this *material* you speak of means. However, no worries. I had considered giving you socks, but I can scrap that plan and go with something plastic."

"He didn't get it," Del said, trying to get comfortable on the lounge.

"Nope," Cupid agreed with a groan.

"Get what?" I demanded. It was getting quite irritating that all these youngsters thought they knew more than me. I was the God of the Sea for the love of everything fishy.

"What is the meaning of Christmas to you?" Rick asked me.

"Is this a trick question?" I inquired wanting to get the answer correct. Games were so much fun especially when I won.

"Nope," Rick said. "No tricks."

"Can I have a hint?" I asked hopefully.

"Nope," Rick said with a grin. "No hints."

"Shite," I mumbled as I began to pace the beach trying to figure out the winning answer.

"Not to worry, Pappy. I shall answer the question," Pirate Doug announced grandly.

"Do you have to?" Cupid asked, pressing the bridge of his nose as if he was in pain.

"Yes!" Pirate Doug replied.

"Wait," I yelled. "If he gets the right answer then I get another question. Otherwise, I will be forced to electrocute everyone."

"Umm… sure," Rick said with a shake of his head. "Pirate Doug, go ahead. Give it a shot."

"I'm terrified right now," Del said with a grin.

"You should be," Cupid chimed in. "We all should be."

Pirate Doug cleared his throat three times, pulled a wedgie from the arse of his breeches and then spoke in his outdoor voice. "Chris was a wonderful scoundrel that I happened upon a few centuries ago when I was running for my life due to banging the sister of the woman I was banging at the time—a real messy situation if you follow my drift. Anyhoo, Chris was wanted by the authorities for running a brothel full of nuns. Of course, you can just imagine how that shite went over. Many a good horny man left that brothel in tears after being castrated by enraged penguins. Poor Chris was simply trying to make a living. The Night of the Holy Tits Carrying Pitchforks was one I will never forget."

"What the fuck?" Keith muttered, completely confused.

"He said *Christmas*, not *Chris*," Del snapped as he punched his brother in the head and sent him flying.

"My bad," Pirate Doug grunted as he got to his feet and rejoined the group.

"I think it would be really good if you didn't talk anymore," Cupid advised Pirate Doug.

"I can do that," Pirate Doug replied with a thumbs up.

"Can you? *Really?*" Del asked.

"No," Pirate Doug admitted. "Absolutely not."

"Alrighty then," Rick said, trying to get the conversation back on track. "Poseidon, what is the meaning of *Christmas* to you?"

"Black Friday?" I answered.

"Nope," Rick said.

"Shite," I muttered and continued to pace the beach. I wondered how many tries I would get before I lost the big showcase. "Phallic Christmas trees?" I tried again.

"May the gods help us all," Del said with a grunt of laughter.

"That's not what I meant," I said quickly, realizing the answer must be incorrect by the confused faces of my men. "Christmas portraits?"

"No," Rick said, opening up a beach chair and getting comfortable. "This is going to take a while."

"Can I have as many guesses as I want?"

"Sure," Rick said. "Although, we're only sticking around for five more minutes."

"I've got it," I shouted. "Presents!"

"Nope," Rick said.

"Are you sure?" I asked.

"I am."

"Positive?" I inquired.

"Very," he replied.

One by one my little army of traitors wandered up to the resort and went back to bed. It was horrifying. I couldn't believe the little shites didn't want to write a letter to Santa Claus when I'd procured the address of the fat bastard.

And what was this *meaning of Christmas* crap? Had I missed something?

Whatever, I was going to write to Santa. If I was to believe Rick, presents were not the real meaning of Christmas. However, I didn't believe Rick at all. He'd clearly misunderstood me. Maybe I should have used the term gift or package. No. A package included a Johnson. The Mermaids had made it abundantly clear that Johnsons were off-limits for Christmas—especially active ones.

The sun would rise soon and I needed a few homing seagulls to fly my letter to the North Pole. There was no time to lose.

Dear Santa,

My name is Poseidon. I'm quite sure you've heard of me. Everyone has. I'm wildly famous.

I have been a very good boy this year. You can ask Wally.

Wally is my she-devil with the outstanding rack if you need confirmation on this. Do not ask Zeus. He is a lying sack of shite.

Please send my regards to Frosty the Snowman. I had no clue you two were banging. The interwebs didn't provide that information. Luckily, I saw the good news on a sweater.

Here is what I want...

It took me three hours, four bottles of rum and twelve pieces of paper, but in the end, it was a masterpiece. I was certain Santa would be impressed.

8

T'WAS THE NIGHT BEFORE
CHRISTMAS

"I'M SO EXCITED," I SANG, DANCING NAKED AROUND OUR suite. "Wally, my lover, spending Christmas on Mystical Isle was the best idea ever. I can't wait for the presents tomorrow morning!"

Wally giggled and shook her head. "Poseidon, you need to calm down and put your diaper on. There are far more important things than presents happening right now."

"What in the salty seas could be more important than *presents?*" I demanded, wondering if I'd forgotten an important holiday ritual. We'd hit Black Friday, tree decorating, Christmas storytime, a holiday portrait on the beach and a letter to Santa. Granted several of the activities had ended in bloodshed, but I still called it a win. The Mermaids had baked lovely Christmas cookies that went wonderfully with rum and everyone had voted to veto caroling. Pirate Doug had a singing voice that could kill… literally. The present exchange would be positively ruined if everyone was dead.

"Petunia has gone into labor," Wally said, clasping her hands together in delight. "We will have a granddaughter very soon—possibly on Christmas morning."

"Wonderful news," I bellowed, putting on a custom-made red and green diaper covered in silver jingle balls. "Do you think I should suggest naming the child Poseidonia Jesus?"

"Umm… no," Wally said with a groan. "I think that would ensure the loss of an important body part."

"Maybe just Poseidonia then?" I suggested.

"Again, nope," Wally said, biting back a laugh.

"It's a beautiful name," I insisted. "It would be such a shame to waste it. However, I will go with what you say and suggest Poseidonacca."

"Mmmkay," Wally said. "I did *not* suggest that. It's awful."

"How about Poseiwallyrica?"

Wally stood, wrapped her arms around me and pressed her delicious lips to mine. For a moment, I couldn't remember my own name. My Wally was a wonder.

"How about we let the children name their own child?" she purred.

"What children? What child?" I asked, confused as I copped a feel of her outstanding arse.

Wally laughed and I happily joined her. I had no clue what was so funny, but her laugh filled my heart with joy.

"Ohhhhh, Wally," I said, grabbing my laptop computer and flopping down on the couch. "I have discovered something wonderful on the interwebs."

"Should I be terrified?" she inquired, seating herself next to me on the divan.

"Not at all," I assured her. "There is a fabulous place to go where you can post every detail of your life no matter how mundane and boring! It's marvelous. I now know what humans eat for dinner and other things that I shouldn't be privy to."

"Please tell me you didn't join," Wally said with a long sigh.

"I can tell you no such thing," I announced. "I've made a page for myself. It's called Poseidon—The Well-Hung God of the Sea. I already have three friends. Well, two. That shite, Zeus, doesn't count."

Wally closed her eyes and pressed her temples. "Zeus is on social media too?"

"Aye," I grunted as I found my page. "Look! I did it all by myself."

Wally's eyes grew wide with what I could only imagine was pride as she scrolled my outstanding page.

"There have to be at least a hundred pictures of you drinking rum," she muttered as she continued to scroll.

"Aye," I said with a wink. "I figured if I put up enough pictures of the good stuff, the companies will send me a few cases—saves me having to pilfer it."

"I see," Wally said, biting down on her lip. "A picture of you wasted in a diaper drinking rum while holding the bottle with your feet might not be the best endorsement."

"Pish," I said with a laugh. "My pecs look wonderful."

"Oh Hades, no," Wally choked out with a wince.

"What?"

"Umm… you put the Christmas family photo up," she pointed out, trying not to laugh.

She failed.

"Aye," I replied and narrowed my eyes at the computer screen. "Do you want to know what that shite-stain Zeus wrote in the comments?"

"No, I do not want to know."

"Well, I'll tell you then. The toga-wearing arsehole asked if he needed to send down cold medicine for all the green boogers in our noses," I griped.

"Did you delete his comment?" Wally asked.

"You can do that?" I asked, amazed. "That probably would have been better than replying."

"You replied?" Wally whispered, paling a bit.

"Aye. Called him a shite-eating mother-humper with a tiny Johnson."

"And how'd that go over?" Wally inquired shaking her head.

"Not well. He's threatened to come down here and kick my arse. But no worries. I have a plan."

"Why does that scare me?" Wally pressed her temples and sighed.

"That Zeus wants to kick my arse?" I asked, confused.

"Nope, that you have a plan."

"Wally, Wally, bo-bally—Bonana-fanna-fo-fally—Fee-fi-mo-mally—Wally!" I sang, pulling the light of my life to her feet and waltzing her across the room. "When have my plans ever gone awry?"

"I can't count that high," she said with a gasp and a giggle as I dipped her.

"Well, this one is sure-fire," I explained. "I'm just going to whip up a little storm off-shore to ensure that Zeus the arsehole can't get to the island. Can't have the shite ruining our perfect Christmas."

Wally squinted at me and pursed her lips. "Just a tiny storm," she advised. "A teeny-tiny storm. If you mess with the weather too much, Mother Nature will be pissed."

I shuddered at the thought. Mother Nature made me look sane.

"A small storm is all we need," I assured her. "Zeus suffers from follicle aquaphobia—cries like a baby if his hair gets mussed. The wanker will turn around and go home if he even sees a drop of rain."

"Are you serious?" Wally asked with a laugh.

"Nay, I'm Poseidon," I replied. "Shall we go take a family photo of Petunia in labor? Might be nice for her to have something with the whole family in it to remember the special day."

"Absolutely not," Wally said, whacking me in the head. "The baby will be enough. Trust me on that."

I trusted my gal with my life but covertly slipped my cell phone into my pocket just in case.

"WHAT IN THE SCALY BARNACLES IS GOING ON?" I ROARED. Looking up at the dark clouds rolling in faster than a soused and overly confident one-legged Pirate in an arse-kicking competition, I choked on my rum. Shiteshiteshite. I'd conjured up a *small* storm, not a fucking typhoon.

"Batten down the hatches," Pirate Doug commanded as

the massive storm continued to roll in from the sea and batter the shores of Mystical Isle.

"Gods durnit," Bonar grunted as he got whacked in the head with a flying beach lounge. "Tis a mutin- minded, crow-bait brewin' on the sea."

"Avast ye," Upton yelled. "All hands on deck. We got a black spot rollin' in. Yar will be dancin' the hempen jig in Davy Jones' locker if ye don't haul arse like a bow-legged bunglar."

"What the hell did he just say?" Keith asked, trying to keep all the beach chairs from flying away.

"No clue," Rick said, turning to Del who appeared frazzled beyond reason. "Del, you don't have to be out here. Go back to Petunia and protect her. The baby could come any time now."

"On it," Del said with a relieved smile as he sprinted back into the resort.

"We're all going to die," Cupid grumbled as he tried to save the large lifeguard towers, only to bet beaned in the head with the massive umbrellas.

"Bad attitude," I said, trying to figure out how in the shite this was happening. "No one is going to bite it. It's Christmas tomorrow."

"Tell that to the hurricane," Cupid said, tackling the tiki bar before it was washed out to sea.

Tallulah raced onto the beach and looked out over the horizon. "We need to get the human guests off the island. That's a mother humper of a storm coming in. Can't risk it."

"Agree," Misty said, joining her sister. "I gathered all the guests into the lobby and gave them vouchers for a free stay in the new year."

"Perfect," Ariel said, grabbing onto a palm tree so she didn't get blown away in the increasingly violent winds. "Who can transport that many humans at the same time?"

"Poseidon can," Misty confirmed.

Madison swam to shore, let her tail morph to legs and sprinted to her sisters. "The dolphins are freaking out," she shouted over the thunder. "Something is off. Are we removing the humans?"

"Yep," Tallulah said, glancing around wildly. "Where in the Seven Seas is Poseidon?"

"Over there fist fighting with himself. Almost knocked himself out cold when he nailed his own head with the rum bottle," Pirate Doug said pointing to me. "Seems very suspicious."

"First smart thing you've said in centuries, darling," Wally commented, patting her son on the head. "Poseidon, get your sorry arse over here or I shall kick it so hard it will be stuck in your mouth."

"Merry Christmas," I bellowed, hoping the sheer volume of my voice might distract from the fact that I was an idiot arsehole and possibly had a teeny-tiny-weeny hand in the vicious storm.

No such luck.

"Fix it," Wally hissed. "This is your fault."

"What?" Tallulah demanded as she got whipped up in a small wind funnel and tossed down the beach.

"I'll save you, my purple hooker," Pirate Doug shouted as

he ran down the beach and narrowly missed getting struck by a giant falling palm tree.

"What does Wally mean this is *your* fault," Madison demanded.

"Zeus said we all had boogers," I began only to be electrocuted by Wally.

"Get to the point before the island blows away," Wally snapped.

"Of course," I said. "Zeus, the small-peckered shite, was coming down to ruin our perfect Christmas so I whipped up a little storm to muss his hair."

"Little?" Tallulah screeched as she rejoined the group and sent a stinging bolt of purple magic my way.

"I might have forgotten to check what Mother Nature had planned for today," I muttered, grabbing a flying tree mid-air and placing it in front of my Johnson since I was fairly sure I was in for a few more electrical surprises.

"*Might have?*" Ariel shouted.

"Alright," I admitted, whacking myself in the head with the tree. "I forgot and I might have been a little soused. This is just awful. I don't know how Santa can get here in a shiteshow like this."

"He did *not* just say he was worried about *Santa*," Tallulah hissed as she began to glow menacingly.

"Aye," Pirate Doug confirmed. "Pappy said exactly that. He found the fat bastard's address on the interwebs and wrote him a letter."

That caused thirty-three seconds of shocked silence as the wild wind howled around us.

"So let me get this straight," Misty said, throwing her

hands in the air. "You created a storm without checking in with Mother Nature that's going to decimate the island because Zeus said we had *boogers?* And the only thing you're worried about is *Santa?*"

"Sounds kind of petty when you put it like that," I volunteered sheepishly.

"How else can I put it?" Misty demanded.

Misty was correct. I was a bad boy—a very bad boy. However, I was also Poseidon the Well- Hung God of the Sea who happened to have Mother Nature on speed dial. Of course, I did point out that her feet were enormous and that she had the slight aroma of dirt last time we'd crossed paths. That had resulted in the loss of a body part on my end. However, the unfortunate exchange had to have been at least fifty years ago.

"I can fix this," I announced, hoping I sounded far more confident than I felt. "Wally, you have enough magic to send the humans back to dry land. Right?"

"I do," Wally said with a curt nod. "I'll take care of it immediately. And you will stop drinking rum before six in the evening."

I must have misunderstood. The wind was howling and shite was flying everywhere. "You want me not to hum during the day?" I questioned.

"No."

"You'd like me to remove my thumb?" I tried again.

"No."

"You think I'm dumb?" I asked.

"Well, yes," Wally said with an eye roll. "But what I said is that you have to stop drinking rum all day long. Your perpetual state of drunkenness has gotten out of control. Look at what you've done."

Shite. Wally was right. Not much was in one piece on the isle except for the lodge. And at the rate the storm was going that might not survive either. Looking around at all the faces I loved, I let my head fall to my chest and I sighed.

"You have my word, my love," I promised Wally.

Wally wrapped her arms around me and hugged me hard as the rain fell in torrents around us. "You are and always will be my hero," she whispered in my ear. "However, if I catch you cheating, I will force you to wear three-piece suits for a century." Snapping her fingers, she disappeared.

My Wally was a she-devil extraordinaire. I would do anything to make the wench happy—even give up my beloved rum. Plus, she was correct. I'd made a tremendous mess out of everything.

"Pappy, you okay?" Pirate Doug asked as he and everyone else watched me warily.

"Never been better, boy," I bellowed… and I meant it. The fact shocked me, but it was true. I was the father to a shiteload of idiots and the father-figure to a shiteload more. I would *not* let my family down. I would save Christmas for my people.

The wind increased and the skies turned black. Debris flew everywhere and I screamed like a girl as Poseidon's Poop Shack got blown out to sea and all of the self-cleaning crockpots along with it. We'd almost died in vain. We would reap no reward from the Black Friday adventure. There would be no gifts that would keep on giving.

"Save the booty," I commanded as I ran to dive into the choppy waters and retrieve the electronics.

"Not so fast," Madison said, tripping me and stepping on my head. "Stop the storm."

"Whoops. My bad," I said, pulling out my cell phone and dialing Mother Nature.

One ring.

Two rings.

Three rings.

Four rings.

Five rings.

Shite, the old hag had better be home or my Johnson was toast.

"What do you want?" Mother Nature hissed into the phone.

"Merry Christmas, Mother Nature… you fabulous piece of… umm… crumbling earth with…umm… wonderfully colossal tootsies," I bellowed. "I need a little favor."

"Who is this?" she snapped.

"Poseidon. The God of the Sea," I replied. I was appalled that I wasn't in her contacts, but had no time to throw a fit.

"You're an ass," she informed me.

"Your point?"

"No point," she said. *"Just an observation."*

"Right. Well, I was wondering if you could tamp back the storm in the Bermuda Triangle?"

"Why?"

"Because Zeus said I had green boogers on social media and the shite doesn't like to mess up his follicles. So naturally, since the arse was trying to hijack my holiday, I created a weeny storm," I explained as a palm tree almost decapitated me.

"*A storm of Johnsons?*" Mother Nature questioned, confused.

"Umm… no," I said, gagging at the visual.

"*Hot dogs?*" she tried again.

"Nay," I said with an eye roll. "A smallish regular storm—no Johnsons have been harmed… yet. However, my Johnson is in danger at the moment. When my teeny storm combined with your storm it became a fucking shiteshow. I realize now that I was entirely too sensitive about Zeus saying I had green boogers."

"*Do you?*" Mother Nature inquired.

"Do I what?"

"*Have boogers?*" she snapped.

"Nay, they were plastic nose plugs," I shouted, defending myself.

"*Is this a new popular style that I'm unaware of?*" Mother Nature demanded.

"Umm… aye. All the rage with the teenagers now," I lied through my teeth. "And I would be honored to send you a large box of green boogers as a token of my thanks and a Christmas gift."

"*Thought you said they weren't boogers,*" Mother Nature said.

"My bad. Nose plugs—made in China," I amended quickly.

There was silence on the other end of the line as the insane old bat considered my offer. I watched in horror as parts of the lodge ripped away from the building and flew through the air. I was ready to get on my knees and beg. Maybe I should facetime the cranky old freak so she could see my appeal for mercy.

"I will take the popular nose plugs and you will visit me and rub my colossal tootsies every Thursday for the next ten years," she said with a cackle.

I only threw up a little bit in my mouth. Rum would be excellent right now, but I'd given Wally my word. Mother Nature drove a hideous and smelly bargain. However, there was no choice.

"Deal," I choked out. "Stop the storm."

"With pleasure. See you next Thursday," she replied as she hung up on me.

And the storm stopped.

But it was too late.

The resort was in shambles.

"Oh my gods," Tallulah gasped out. "Petunia, Wally and Del are in there."

"Please let everyone be okay," I mumbled as I shot like a ball out of a cannon toward the ruined resort. "Please."

9

LET THE SHITESHOW COMMENCE

"WE'RE FINE," WALLY INSISTED AS I RAN AROUND TRYING TO find something that would work as a bed for Petunia. "Del created a magic bubble around us as the resort blew away. It was quite impressive. Not a scratch on any of us."

"Del, you can have my scepter and my designer diaper collection," I said, still trying to find a pillow and blanket.

"Umm… thank you, Pappy, but no. I'm good," Del said with a chuckle as he held a very grumpy Petunia in his arms.

"I'll take your scepter," Petunia announced. "But just so you know, once I blow this baby out, I'm going to shove it up your ass."

"Fair enough," I said, handing over the royal scepter. "I deserve no less. In fact, all of you can pick an item to shove up my arse. We can have an arse-shoving party after we open our gif…" I stopped and almost passed out in horror.

There were no gifts. There was no decorated tree. No cookies. No self-cleaning crockpots or pretzel makers with cheese warmers. No weenie toasters. We had lost all the Johnson and knocker sweaters as well—not that anyone would wear them again since the boys' sweaters were covered in blood. Not even one damned green booger was left either. I'd have to order a new case for Mother Enormous Feet.

"Poseidon, don't cry," Tallulah said, patting me on the head gently. "It's okay. It's just stuff. The good thing is that everyone is fine. We got all the humans to safety and no one on the isle died. We're all alive to be able to shove stuff up your arse."

"Yes, yes, yes," I said. "That is outstanding. But where will Petunia give birth? Do you think there's any room at an inn on a neighboring island?"

"Nope," Madison said with a shrug. "No room at any inn right now. It's Christmas. Everything is full."

"What will we do? Should I pop over to another island and go from inn to inn looking for a vacancy?" I demanded as I swatted at a goat who was trying to eat my diaper. "Why are there puppies, kitties, goats and deer here?"

"My zoo," Rick said, checking his animals over carefully. "Looks like everyone made it."

Bonar and Upton approached the group and raised their hands politely.

"Yes?" Tallulah asked with a tired smile. "Do you have something to say?"

"Aye, lassie. I do," Upton said with a gallant bow that looked like he was squatting to take a dump.

Thankfully, he wasn't. However, the goats were not nearly as couth.

Upton righted his Pirate hat and went on. "Bonar, Kim, Yolanda and meself have constructed a shanty on the beach with some of the scurvy wreckage."

"Did you find any self-cleaning crockpots?" I inquired only to get punched in the head by Wally.

"Nay, no crockpots, yar Majesty," Bonar said. "But methinks it would be a fine place to bring a wee one into the world."

"I'll gather some seagrass to put on the ground," Rick said, grabbing Madison's hand and darting off to find it.

"I think I can whip up a cradle with this rope and wood," Cupid said.

"I can find some sarong scraps for a blanket," Misty volunteered as she and Cupid quickly wandered away.

"Umm… you do realize what this is sounding like?" Wally inquired with a giggle. "We've even got the animals."

Tallulah laughed. "Correct. However, we will not be showing up late and bringing gold, frankincense and myrrh."

"So right you are," Ariel said, grinning. "I say we help deliver the little bugger, find some food and get the area nice and clean."

"Wise women are *way* better than wise men," Wally pointed out as she and the gals gently helped Petunia over to the shanty.

"Can I have a non-virgin pina colada after the little Vega arrives?" Petunia inquired with a pained grunt of laughter.

"Absolutely," Del said, following his love and the other gals. "You can have anything your heart desires."

"I love you, Del," Petunia said over her shoulder. "But if

you ever knock me up again, I will hack off your Johnson with a dull butter knife."

"That's wonderful, darling," Del said with a grin.

"I think my boy has lost it," I muttered as I watched the small group move toward the simple shanty on the beach.

"Nay," Pirate Doug said, giving me a wink. "My brother is in love with a Mermaid. One hundred percent in love. If Tallulah wanted to lop my salami off, I'd let her."

"Are you daft?" I demanded.

"Nay," Pirate Doug answered. "It would grow back and I would do anything for my purple hooker."

"Don't call me a hooker," Tallulah yelled back at him.

"Whoops. My bad," Pirate Doug shouted. "I meant purple swimming hooker."

"Does anyone know what they were talking about—the gold, frank and beans and something else?" I asked.

"I think it's the name of some kind of fancy beer to go with the frank and beans," Keith informed us.

"Possibly." I nodded. Keith might not be as idiotic as I'd always believed.

"Nay, no clue what they meant," Pirate Doug said. "But I say we just nod, smile and do whatever they say."

"Good deal," Keith agreed.

"Yar Majesty," Upton said, handing me his spyglass. "Ye might want to take a gander out to sea."

"Why?" I asked, raising the glass to my eye. "Shite."

"That's why," Upton said. "Do ye want me to take the ship out and save his arse?"

"Nay," I said, making sure my diaper was secure. I'd hate to lose it in the salty sea. The jingle balls made such a lovely noise. "Pretty sure you don't have a ship anymore after the storm. And that arse out there drowning in the ocean is mine."

"There's a floating arse in the ocean?" Pirate Doug asked, grabbing the spyglass and scanning the horizon.

"Aye," I said. "However, the entire body is attached to the arse and his hair is a disaster. I want you men waiting on shore with your cameras ready."

"Why?" Keith asked.

"Blackmail," I said with a laugh. "He made fun of my boogers on social media. I will now make fun of his hair."

Sprinting out to the water's edge, I dove in and felt right at home. The ocean fed my spirit and calmed my soul.

"Where are you going?" Wally called out. "The baby is coming soon."

"Have to save Zeus," I called back to my gal.

"Do NOT kick his arse," Wally warned. "No time for shenanigans."

"Roger that," I yelled right before I dove deep and swam faster than any fish in the sea.

I might not kick his arse, but I would certainly scare the shite out of him. He'd do no less to me.

"You're a son-of-a-bitch," Zeus snapped as I dragged his soggy arse ashore.

"Tell me something I don't know," I muttered with a laugh as I dropped my fellow god in the sand. "Get your shots boys."

Pirate Doug and Keith quickly sniped a few pictures of Zeus not looking his best. His ire was a pure delight. Not only was this payback for saying I had green boogers on social media, but the shite had wedgied me in front of all the other gods at a team-building summit last summer. It had taken me an hour to remove my diaper from my arse. The fucker was strong. Although, the awe-shocked and impressed faces of the other gods when my left nard fell out of the diaper almost made it worth it. My marbles were enormous.

"Thank you for saving me," Zeus said in a tone so soft I wasn't sure I heard him correctly.

"What?" I inquired with a grin.

"You heard me, you idiot," he griped.

"I did, old man," I replied, taking his hand and pulling him to his feet. "And I'm sorry I had the boys take pictures of your hair."

"You'll delete them?" Zeus asked.

"Nay. Of course not. It will keep you in line for a few centuries," I told him with a wink. "However, I would like to invite you to Christmas dinner with my family."

"We don't have any Christmas dinner, dumbass," Tallulah shouted from the shanty.

"Shite," I muttered.

"How about we fish for dinner?" Zeus suggested.

"Sounds good," Tallulah shouted as Petunia grunted in pain and threatened every Johnson on the isle.

"Is everything alright?" Zeus asked, concerned as he covered his jewels with his hands.

"Aye," I told him, following suit. "I have a granddaughter about to be born. Would you like to watch?"

"Are you freaking kidding me?" Petunia screeched. "I will kill you so dead if you step one foot into my shanty. You feel me?"

"Aye," I said, grabbing Zeus, Pirate Doug, Keith, Cupid, Rick, Upton and Bonar by the scruffs of their necks and dragging them to relative safety. "Come on, men. We're going to fish for dinner."

"I'm vegan," Rick reminded me.

"I'm vegetarian," Keith added.

"And seaweed," I added with an eye roll. "Our Johnsons are not safe here."

"What about Del?" Pirate Doug asked.

"Del's Johnson is fair game," I told my idiot son. "As will yours be when you have a child."

"Roger that," Pirate Doug said. "Umm... is that a self-cleaning crockpot I spy?"

Whipping around, I gasped with joy. "Aye and I believe I see the schlong shaped cake pan as well. Boys, we're after fish, seaweed and electronics. We might just have a Christmas after all. Let's GO!"

10

YES, POSEIDON... THERE IS A SANTA CLAUS

"It's a healthy baby girl. She's gorgeous and looks just like her mamma," Del shouted with joy as he danced on the beach under the full moon. "I'm a fucking father! Best damned day of my life."

"Congratulations," Zeus said, snapping his fingers and producing celebratory cigars. "It's terrifyingly wonderful to hear that Poseidon's family tree continues to grow."

"I'll take one of those cigars," Wally said, joining the group of men on the beach. "Petunia was a goddess. Cussed like a wasted sailor and blew that baby out on the third push. Her primal screaming was outstanding. Pretty sure all of our eardrums were perforated. It's truly wonderful to be Immortal and have outstanding healing powers or we'd all be deaf. Of course, the birth was a bloody, violent mess, but I was proud of Del for only passing out twice."

The men paled and our eyes grew huge. I was delighted that we'd been fishing during the birth of my granddaughter. Whoever thought that men should run the world was gravely mistaken. Women had much larger nards than we did any day of the week.

"The goats were a poor choice of birthing companions though," Wally went on as she lit up her cigar. "The one called Nancy felt she needed to add to the ruckus and sang the song of her people throughout the entire birth. Not to mention, she pooped a small nugget mountain in the shanty. But Petunia enjoyed having a screaming competition partner so I let the goat stay."

"It was amazing," Del announced with tears in his eyes. "Petunia threatened my Johnson in many creative and horrifying ways, but I'm sure she didn't mean it."

"Yes, I did," Petunia called out from the shanty. "But I love you."

"Love you too," Del yelled as he sprinted back to the shanty to get his mate and his baby girl.

"It's after midnight," Cupid pointed out. "Merry Christmas everyone."

"Merry Christmas," Pirate Doug bellowed as he pieced together some wood to make a table for the midnight feast. "Are you dingleberries hungry?"

"Yes," Wally said as she zapped her beloved son with a bolt of lightning. "And don't ever call me a dingleberry again. I'll get the gals."

"Shite," Pirate Doug muttered, rubbing his smoldering backside. "I thought dingleberry was better than hooker."

"You thought wrong," Rick said as he placed a platter of seaweed salad on the rickety table. The platter was made from the leftover innards of a beach umbrella, but it worked in a pinch.

We'd caught fish and shrimp for the feast and cooked them over a roaring bonfire on the beach. Everyone did their part and it was wonderfully bonding. The electronics we'd fished out of the sea were useless. However, I'd insisted that we put them under the makeshift Christmas tree that Keith and Ariel had cobbled together. It was decorated with several green plastic boogers, some shiny sea glass and a few shells. A starfish that Baby Thornycraft and Neville had found sat atop the masterpiece.

"Here we go," Cupid announced, placing a huge piece of driftwood on the table loaded down with perfectly grilled delicacies. "*Bon appetit.*"

"Ladies first," Tallulah said, walking a radiant Petunia with her babe in her arms to the front of the line.

"May I?" I asked, glancing down at the swaddled child.

"You may," Petunia said with a wide grin as she handed me the precious bundle.

My heart pounded furiously in my chest and my eyes filled with salty tears as I stared into the eyes of the perfect little child. She wrinkled her tiny nose, smiled at me then blew a toot from her bottom that filled me with wonder and pride. I had no clue something so tiny could fart so loud.

"She's perfect," I announced, handing the babe to her father.

I wasn't exactly sure if it was an outstanding toot or a vigorous poop that the little beauty had just produced. I wasn't good at changing diapers except for my own. So, on the outside chance that the rule was whoever held the babe when she took a dump had to change said dump, I handed her back to Del.

"I'm starving," Petunia said with a giggle. "I've had a busy day."

"Aye," I said, handing her a broken coconut shell to put her food in. "You have made me proud, little Mermaid."

"Thank you," Petunia replied grinning. "I'm pretty proud of me too."

"As you should be," Wally said, handing her a stick to spear her food with. "It has been a perfect Christmas."

Had it? There were no presents. We were eating on the beach with makeshift plates and cutlery. There were no toys for the children and no self-cleaning crockpots for the women. All my plans had been washed away in the storm that was of my own doing. I felt terrible.

"Stop that, Poseidon," Wally admonished as she handed me a coconut shell filled with delicious food. "Look around at our family and tell me what you see."

Following my love's directive so I didn't get electrocuted, I scanned the beach and took it all in. Ariel and Keith were laughing and playing tag with Baby Thornycraft and Neville. Upton and Yolanda were creating a Christmas sandcastle masterpiece as Rick and Madison clapped and took picture after picture.

"They're happy," I whispered as I continued to watch my lovely family.

"Very," Wally confirmed taking my hand in hers.

Petunia sat with Del on the remnants of a lounge chair as Tallulah and Pirate Doug oohed and ahhed over the newest addition to my line.

Zeus was in deep discussion with Bonar and Kim and appeared not to understand a word the Pirate said. Bonar didn't notice and went on with a story that had his mate, Kim, in stitches.

"No one died. It's a fucking miracle," Cupid yelled gleefully as he took Misty into his arms and danced her around the beach to the delight of everyone.

"You see?" Wally whispered as she leaned her head on my shoulder. "It's not about the gifts. It's about family and love."

"Aye," I replied with content, stroking her long curly locks. "You are correct as usual, my love."

"Incoming," Upton shouted, pointing out at the sea.

"What the hell is that?" Cupid asked, squinting his eyes and trying to make out what was flying toward us.

"Shite," Pirate Doug bellowed. "I have no clue. Arm yourselves everyone. We're under attack."

As the Mermaids and their mates gathered weapons, I slowly walked to the water's edge and began to laugh. Who would have guessed?

"Nay," I bellowed to my family. "Put down your weapons. Our visitor comes in peace."

"Who is it?" Tallulah asked as she joined me.

Looking down at her, I grinned. "You're not going to believe me, little Mermaid."

"Try me," she shot back.

"It's Santa."

"He's real? Are you shitting me?" Tallulah asked with a laugh.

"I shite you not," I replied. "Move the table and clear the

beach. We must create a landing area for Santa Claus!"

"W AIT," I SAID, CONFUSED. "A RE YOU THE *REAL* S ANTA?"

"As a matter of fact, Poseidon, I am," the jolly fat bastard said as he enjoyed an enormous coconut shell filled with shrimp and seaweed.

His reindeer were grazing with the goats and his sled was parked sideways in the sand. I was curious if the rotund man had enjoyed a few spiked eggnogs before he'd arrived. His landing was positively embarrassing. However, I said not a word about the fact that he'd basically ejected himself from his sleigh due to flying in upside down. Upton and Bonar had quickly and efficiently procured Santa from a palm tree and everyone politely pretended they hadn't witnessed the crash landing.

"Then who are all the mall Santas?" Tallulah inquired as she set Santa up with a pina colada.

"They're all me," Santa replied, chuckling.

"How is that possible?" Petunia asked with her babe sleeping soundly in her arms.

"Can you keep a secret?" Santa asked.

"Yes!" I announced. "But a quick question. Would it be okay if I put it on social media?"

I was electrocuted by the Mermaids from all sides, so I took that as a no.

"I'm an alien—from Uranus who relocated with Mrs. Claus to the North Pole. The climate is very similar," Santa whispered as his eyes twinkled with delight. "Once a year, I splice my DNA into millions of pieces and send them all over the land. It's a bit dicey for Mrs. Claus since I'm a randy old bastard, but she enjoys the variety."

No one quite knew what to say to that one… except Pirate Doug.

"Did you just say you're from my anus?" my dolt of a son inquired. Although, I had to admit the same question had crossed my mind as well.

"No, I said Uranus," Santa clarified.

"My anus?" Pirate Doug asked again, completely perplexed.

"Nope. Uranus," Santa said.

Pirate Doug glanced around in horror and confusion. "Thank you for explaining, Santa."

"You are most welcome and now you know," Santa said as he downed his drink and then pressed the area between his bushy eyebrows in pain. "Mother-elf-humper, I have a brain-freeze."

"You okay?" I asked, concerned. We certainly wouldn't want to accidentally kill Santa, even though he was under the mistaken impression that he lived in our arses.

"I'm fine," he said, back to being jolly. "Could I get another one of those?"

"Only if you promise to drink it slowly," Tallulah said with a laugh as she handed the old coot another.

"Promise," Santa replied with a wink. "I came here today because I received a letter that warmed my heart."

"And your anus?" Pirate Doug questioned.

"Umm… nope. Just my heart," Santa said. "I would like to read it to you."

"Ahhhhh," I said, trying to remember who I'd insulted in my letter. As far as I could recall, it was only Zeus, which was fine. "Is it my letter?"

"It is!" Santa replied with a delighted chuckle. "I haven't gotten a letter from someone who understood the true meaning of Christmas in a very long time. It made me get into my sleigh and fly to the Mystical Isle."

"So you don't use the sleigh much?" Ariel asked with a giggle.

"I don't," Santa admitted with a cheerful grin. "Been sighted so many times by Air Traffic Control that I usually leave the driving to someone else. However, it is Christmas and my clones are quite busy."

"Are you saying that Poseidon understands the true meaning of Christmas?" Wally asked with a huge grin on her lovely face. "My Poseidon?"

"That is exactly what I'm saying," Santa said. "Would you like to hear the letter?"

"Absolutely," Cupid said with a baffled expression on his face.

"Then gather 'round and make yourselves comfortable," Santa instructed. "Although, I'd like to point out before I start that I'm not banging Frosty the Snowman."

"Sorry about that," I said sheepishly.

"Not to worry," Santa said. "Frosty was amused. His wife was not."

"Shite," I muttered, hoping Mrs. Frosty wasn't the vengeful type. "Oh, and you can skip the part about Zeus being a lying sack of shite."

"Thank you," Zeus said with an eye roll. "Please, Santa, don't leave *anything* out."

I was a little—or a lot—soused when I'd penned my letter, but I'd written from my heart. I just hoped my grammar wasn't too shitey.

And Santa began to read...

"Dear Santa,

My name is Poseidon. I'm quite sure you've heard of me. Everyone has. I'm wildly famous.

I have been a very good boy this year. You can ask Wally. Wally is my she-devil with the outstanding rack if you need confirmation on this. Do not ask Zeus. He is a lying sack of shite.

Please send my regards to Frosty the Snowman. I had no clue you two were banging. The interwebs didn't provide that information. Luckily, I saw the good news on a sweater.

Here is what I want...

For my mate Wally, I would like to make her laugh every day for the rest of her life. She is my reason for living and her happiness is my happiness.

For Ariel and Keith, I wish health, happiness and joy. Ariel's giggle lights up my world and I want to keep it that way. Keith isn't the sharpest tool in the shed, but he takes my side in most disputes and I admire his nards.

For Misty, Cupid and Baby Thornycraft, I wish them the ability to spread love through the Universe and make it a better place. Their hearts are wondrous and they deserve all the joys that love has to offer. While Cupid is an arse occasionally, I still love the shite.

For Madison and Rick, I wish many dangerous and delightful missions. I wish for them to always come home safe and sound. The world would not be half as beautiful without them in it.

For Petunia and Del, I wish a healthy baby and millions of years of happiness. I am proud to have my Genie son back in my life and hope to make him proud of me as well. Petunia and Del have been through the wringer and it's their turn to shine.

For Upton and Yolanda and Bonar and Kim, I wish joy and laughter throughout Immortality. I also wish for grammar lessons for the Pirates. And for little Neville, I wish strength and wisdom. He will lead the Gnomes someday and I know he will be just and kind.

For Tallulah and Pirate Doug, I wish every happiness in the Universe. Someday my idiot son will take my place on the throne and I am wildly overjoyed that Tallulah will kick his arse if the little shite gets out of line.

For the gods on Mount Olympus, I wish they would finally admit that my Johnson is far superior to theirs. However, I also wish them good health and joy in life... but more joy if they will accept that my salami is higher ranking than theirs.

And for myself? I wish for nothing. I already have everything that I want. Love, laughter and family.

Thank you for your time, you fat bastard.

xoxo Poseidon—The Well-Hung God of the Sea"

The silence was deafening. Had I written a bad letter? Was everyone angry? Did I miss the real meaning of Christmas again? Shite. Maybe writing from my heart was a dreadful idea. It was after six, so I could have some rum. I could just go for a quick swim and then drown my embarrassment in alcohol.

"Oh my gods," Wally cried out as she tackled me and

kissed my face all over. "That was the most beautiful letter I've ever heard."

"Did you like the part about my Johnson being the best?" I asked with a laugh, wrapping my arms around her.

"Umm… not my favorite part, but it was good," Wally told me.

"Hug my pappy!" Pirate Doug bellowed as I was lovingly attacked my family.

The kisses, hugs, backslaps and happy tears were the best gifts I could have received. Screw the self-cleaning crockpots. However, I would be pilfering one of those soon for Wally. She deserved it.

"I have an announcement to make," Del said, clearing his throat and getting the attention of all. "We have chosen a name for our daughter."

"I thought it was Vega," Tallulah said as she gave me one last hug and got to her feet.

"It is," Petunia confirmed with a secretive smile on her lips. "However, Vega has a middle name."

"Out with it," I bellowed, tickling Baby Thornycraft and Neville. "We need to celebrate little Vega's birth."

"Tell him," Petunia said, nudging Del.

"I thought you wanted to tell him," Del said, kissing the top of Petunia's head.

"I did," she said. "But now I want you to tell him. He's your father."

"Somebody just tell me," I said, getting a bit alarmed.

Del again cleared his throat and stepped forward. "In honor of the wonderfully loving freak who had a hand in bringing most of us together… we have decided to name our daughter Vega Poseidonia in honor of her grandfather, Poseidon."

The tears were copious. The joyful screaming was out of control. Why was everyone so insane? Wait. It was me. I was screaming. I was crying. My family simply watched me quietly and somewhat warily with radiant smiles on their faces.

"Is this true?" I choked out through my tears.

"It is," Wally said, taking my hands in hers. "You're a nutjob, but you are a very loved nutjob."

"I'll take it," I whispered as the family dispersed and wandered back to the resort that Santa had magically restored with his alien anus power.

Of course, Santa was staying with us until Mrs. Claus could get down here and drive the sleigh back home. Tallulah had insisted when Mrs. Claus arrived that both she and Santa stay for a well-deserved vacation. Santa was delighted with the plan.

"You ready to go to bed?" Wally asked with a happy sigh.

"I was thinking I would sit on the beach for a bit, look at the stars and indulge in a bit of rum," I told her.

"Then I shall join you," she replied.

"You will?" I asked with a chuckle.

"Your happiness is my happiness, Poseidon," Wally said. "It always has been and it always will be."

"Do I still have to go to Jazzercize with you?" I inquired casually, pushing my luck.

"Yep," Wally said with a giggle. "I like to ogle your pecs when I exercise."

I puffed up with pride. My pecs were outstanding. "Then I would be delighted to join you."

"Let's spend Christmas here every year," Wally said as we got comfortable in the sand.

Aye, my love," I said, wrapping my arms around her. "Tis a wonderful idea."

I'd meant what I'd said in my letter. I truly did have everything I wanted—love, laughter and family. They were the things that gold coins or human credit cards couldn't buy.

"Should we wish on a star?" I asked, pulling Wally closer.

"Not tonight," Wally whispered, laying her head on my shoulder. "Save them for another time. All of my wishes have come true today."

I glanced up at the sky and smiled. The stars twinkled and winked. I winked right back at them and sighed with pure contentment.

Wally was correct. Our wishes had indeed been granted and the love of my Immortal life was at my side. Life didn't get much better.

Merry Christmas to all… and to all a good night.

The End

ROBYN'S BOOK LIST
(IN CORRECT READING ORDER)

HOT DAMNED SERIES
Fashionably Dead
Fashionably Dead Down Under
Hell on Heels
Fashionably Dead in Diapers
A Fashionably Dead Christmas
Fashionably Hotter Than Hell
Fashionably Dead and Wed
Fashionably Fanged
Fashionably Flawed
A Fashionably Dead Diary
Fashionably Forever After
Fashionably Fabulous
A Fashionable Fiasco
Fashionably Fooled
Fashionably Dead and Loving It
Fashionably Dead and Demonic

The Oh My Gawd Couple

GOOD TO THE LAST DEATH SERIES
It's a Wonderful Midlife Crisis
Whose Midlife Crisis Is It Anyway?
A Most Excellent Midlife Crisis
My Midlife Crisis, My Rules
You Light Up My Midlife Crisis
It's A Matter of Midlife and Death
The Facts of Midlife

MY SO CALLED MYSTICAL MIDLIFE SERIES
The Write Hook
You May Be Write
All the Write Moves

SHIFT HAPPENS SERIES
Ready to Were
Some Were in Time
No Were To Run
Were Me Out
Were We Belong

MAGIC AND MAYHEM SERIES
Switching Hour
Witch Glitch
A Witch in Time
Magically Delicious
A Tale of Two Witches
Three's A Charm

Switching Witches
You're Broom or Mine?
The Bad Boys of Assjacket
The Newly Witch Game

SEA SHENANIGANS SERIES
Tallulah's Temptation
Ariel's Antics
Misty's Mayhem
Petunia's Pandemonium
Jingle Me Balls

A WYLDE PARANORMAL SERIES
Beauty Loves the Beast

HANDCUFFS AND HAPPILY EVER AFTERS SERIES
How Hard Can it Be?
Size Matters
Cop a Feel

If after reading all the above you are still wanting more adventure and zany fun, read *Pirate Dave and His Randy Adventures*, the romance novel budding novelist Rena helped wicked Evangeline write in *How Hard Can It Be?*

Warning: Pirate Dave Contains Romance Satire, Spoofing, and Pirates with Two Pork Swords.

NOTE FROM THE AUTHOR

If you enjoyed reading *Jingle Me Balls*, please consider leaving a positive review or rating on the site where you purchased it. Reader reviews help my books continue to be valued by resellers and help new readers make decisions about reading them.

You are the reason I write these stories and I sincerely appreciate each of you!

Many thanks for your support,
~ Robyn Peterman

Want to hear about my new releases?
Join my newsletter!

MORE IN THIS SERIES

SEA SHENANIGANS

Visit robynpeterman.com for more info!

ABOUT ROBYN PETERMAN

Robyn Peterman writes because the people inside her head won't leave her alone until she gives them life on paper. Her addictions include laughing really hard with friends, shoes (the expensive kind), Target, iced coffee with a squirt of chocolate syrup in a Yeti cup, bejeweled reading glasses, her kids, her super-hot hubby and collecting stray animals.

A former professional actress with Broadway, film and T.V. credits, she now lives in the South with her family and too many animals to count.

Writing gives her peace and makes her whole, plus having a job where she can work in her sweatpants works really well for her.

EXCERPT FROM: TALLULAH'S TEMPTATION

This is an excerpt from Book 1 of the
Sea Shenanigans series by Robyn Peterman.

Grab your copy here!

CHAPTER ONE

CHAPTER 1

Pirate Doug

"Doug, this is an offer you would be foolish to refuse," Renee said, running a hand through her curly red hair in frustration.

"*Pirate* Doug," I reminded her for the fourth time. If the human woman—as attractive and beddable as she was— couldn't be bothered to remember my title, I couldn't be bothered to listen.

I was an extremely busy Vampire Pirate of the High Seas. Being on the run for my life was a full fucking time job. Sitting still in an office on dry land was making me itchy. I was a sitting duck for my inordinately long list of enemies. Of course killing me was an almost impossible feat, but I could be dismembered quite easily by the right foe. My arms and legs would regenerate, but it really pissed me off to have to regrow the appendages—not to mention dry socket sucked. I'd had the same legs for three hundred years and I planned on keeping it that way. Now my arms were an entirely different story. Taking a week off to sprout new limbs was a dangerous proposition for someone as *in demand* as I was.

"So let me get this straight," I said, casing the office for something to abscond with. Sadly, there was nothing shiny in sight. Either Renee had hidden all her precious booty or she didn't have any. "You're going to pay off my debts if I agree to take this appalling offer I have yet to hear?"

"No," she said with a barely disguised eye roll. "No one in their right mind would pay off your astronomical and wildly illegal financial woes."

"So then I'm wasting my time and risking my life by being here," I said, standing up to take my leave.

"Sit," Renee commanded in a voice that made me a bit randy and resulted in my breeches growing tight.

The small woman had large balls. I found her rudeness wildly arousing. Not that I would make a play for the owner of the Otherworld Defense Agency. She was mated to two Werewolves. Those hairy bastards were vicious. Besides, I preferred nonhuman women who enjoyed the sea—much more durable in the boudoir on my ship.

"Your debt is insurmountable," she pointed out.

"Thank you," I replied with a gallant bow.

"That wasn't a compliment," she said, biting back a grin.

"My bad," I said with my most charming smile.

I was obnoxiously aware that I was an obscenely good looking bastard. It had come in handy over my many centuries. Pretty people could get away with murder—not that I was into that sort of thing. I was far more into price-less objects, rare artifacts and getting laid on a very regular basis. Murder only came into play when someone was gunning for my sexy ass.

"Doug," she began.

"*Pirate* Doug."

"Right. *Pirate Doug*," Renee amended with a shake of her head and a chuckle. "I can have the most egregious bounty removed from your idiot head if you take the job."

"You can get the Gnomes off my arse?" I inquired, surprised. I let the *idiot* comment go mostly because it was accurate and the rest of her statement was very intriguing.

Gnomes were the bane of my fabulous existence at the moment. The bald bastards were after me for too many reasons to count. Of course bedding the gal pal of their head honcho a decade ago didn't help, but draining their international bank accounts was certainly high on their list of my transgressions as well.

"They owe us a favor or seven," she said cryptically. "We can erase what you've done. However, I'd like to suggest that you steer clear of the Gnomes in the future."

"Could you be more specific?" I inquired. Implied rules and vague hints were not my forte.

"Sure," she replied with a sigh and then a laugh. "Keep your dick in your pants and stop stealing their shit. Period. We can't negate your future crimes—only the ones you've already committed."

"Interesting," I said, running my hand over my well-trimmed goatee and considering this offer although I still had no idea what I had to do. I was tempted to say yes even though the mission was a mystery. I'd had far too many close calls of late. It was getting quite tiresome to have to fight off those bloodthirsty Gnome sons of bitches.

There were plenty of people and species to steal from. I could avoid looting the Gnomes for a few hundred years. However, keeping my man tool in my breeches might prove to be difficult. The female Gnomes adored me. They were animals in the sack and delightfully violent—all attributes that made my roger quite jolly. Although, living to see tomorrow did appeal...

"Let's say... *hypocritically*, I accept your offer. What exactly did you have in mind?" I asked, sitting back down, but rearranging my chair so I could see the exit clearly. Never good to let someone sneak up from behind. That's how I'd lost my left arm three months ago.

"I'm sorry, what did you just say?" Renee asked, seemingly confused. "Do you mean hypothetically?"

I paused in thought. I had been told it made me look smarter...

"No. I'm fairly sure I'm a hypocrite. Did I use it in the sentence wrong? I have a word of the day calendar and I've been trying to stretch the old vocabulary. I've found pretending to have a higher IQ gets me laid more regularly."

The human woman was stunned to silence for a brief moment and then had an alarming coughing fit that caused her face to turn a bright red—or possibly she was choking to death. No matter. She was clearly bowled over by my brains and brawn. I was gorgeous and had a legendary trouser snake. However, if she keeled over in my presence

I'd have to answer to the fucking Werewolves. That was not my idea of a good time.

"Do you need me to hemlock you?" I inquired politely.

Her eyes grew wide and I wondered if she was daft. I'd heard quite the opposite, but her behavior was strange.

"Umm... no," she said, getting control of herself with effort. "That won't be necessary."

"Very well then," I replied. "What are the terms?"

"You still have your ship?" she asked, wiping a few tears from her eyes as she cleared her throat several times.

"I have a fleet," I replied proudly.

"Do I want to know how you amassed a fleet?"

I paused and winked at the harried woman. "Probably not."

"Fine," Renee said, scrubbing her hand over her mouth to hide her grin. "We've received a distress call from a Mermaid pod in the Bermuda Triangle. They're being attacked by Sea Hags."

I froze for a brief moment. Mermaids were my weakness —well, one Mermaid in particular, but she wanted to off my fine ass. Whatever, I didn't need that delectable swimming hooker. She'd had her chance. It was completely irrelevant that *I'd* fucked it up.

"And this is a problem?" I asked, not clear on why anyone would want to save either of those species.

"*Yes*, it's a problem," Renee said. "Mermaids are good and Sea Hags are not."

"Not sure where you're getting your Intel, but the last Mermaid I encountered tried to castrate me. Do you have any clue how long it takes to grow back a schlong?"

Again the poor human was rendered mute. I really didn't know how she ran a business if she couldn't hold a decent conversation.

"Well, do you?" I demanded.

"No," she choked out and then narrowed her eyes. "And I can live out the rest of my life without knowing. The mission is to help the Mermaids fight off the Sea Hags. While your intellect is debatable, your skills are unrivaled. This is why I'm offering you the mission. If you can't do it, fine. We're done here."

Renee stood up and offered me her hand. This was not going my way. I hated when things didn't go my way. I usually threw an epic fit, but somehow didn't think that would go over too well right now. And I wasn't quite sure if she'd just insulted me.

What I *needed* was to get the fucking Gnomes off my arse. So what if I had to help some legless wenches. If I wore a protective codpiece over my Johnson, I would probably be fine. As long as it wasn't the Mystical Isle Pod… I'd be a dead Pirate walking with those waterlogged, sexy freaks of nature.

"Wait," I said, ignoring her outstretched hand. "So what you're saying is that I need to send the Sea Hags to Davy Jones' locker—or at least make a few Black Spots to scare the heinous scallywags off the water loving, scaly tailed bitches' arses? However, I'd like to know if hornswoggling is off the table, from what I understand the Sea Hags have impressive booty."

"Umm… I think so," Renee said, trying to decipher my statement. "If that means you'll stop the Sea Hags from killing the Mermaids and stealing their land—then yes. Pretty sure you don't think the Hags have nice asses, so I'll assume you're inquiring if you can loot their treasures?"

I always forgot that most didn't speak Pirate. However, the human woman was right on the money.

"Yes," I replied with a grin.

She shook her head and closed her eyes. "If you steal from the Sea Hags, I don't want to know about it. However, there will be no stealing from the Mermaids."

"Deal," I said, taking her small hand in mine and shaking it. "Piece of cake. And what is the pod of man-eating Mermaids called?"

There were hundreds of those tail wagging swimming hookers in the Bermuda Triangle. There was no way in Hell it could be the one pod that wanted me strung up and beheaded.

"It's the Mystical Isle Pod. Do you know of them?"

It was now my turn to be speechless. The prospect of seeing the one that got away—or rather, the one who tried to castrate me for a slight misunderstanding—was horrifyingly tempting. If I declined the job on the outside chance that I would lose my pecker, I'd have to deal with the Gnomes. The Gnomes could mean actual death for me. Weighing the cost of my dong against the cost of my life took me a few minutes.

I smiled at Renee so she wouldn't be alerted to my inner terror and turmoil. Deciding to risk my wanker as opposed to my life, I nodded and widened my smile. I prayed to Poseidon that it didn't resemble a constipated wince.

"I do know of them," I replied, nodding slowly and

slightly bent at the waist already in mourning for my nads. "Haven't seen those gals in a century. It shall be jolly to get reacquainted."

"Are you sure?" she asked, eyeing me strangely.

"Positive," I answered. "Absolutely positive."

Positive that this was a very *bad* move on my part. Tallulah, the leader of the vicious Mystical Isle Pod of Mermaids, wasn't exactly fond of me... and that was putting it mildly. The horrible, sexy, breathtaking woman had been starring in my dreams for too many years to count. Sadly, just when my mind wandered to the really *good nookie part,* the dream ended with her whacking my Johnson off. I just hoped to Hell and back that the Sea Hags had some outstanding booty. If I was going to have to regrow my tallywhacker, the treasure had better damn well be good.

CPSIA information can be obtained
at www.ICGtesting.com
Printed in the USA
LVHW101946181022
730978LV00002B/400